AMAZON BESTSELLING AUTHOR
XAVIER NEAL
can't match this

1

can't
match
this

Can't Match This
By Xavier Neal
©Xavier Neal 2019
Cover by Angie Merriam
All Rights Reserved

Subscribe to my newsletter!
http://eepurl.com/bYqwLf

Table of Contents

Dedication:

To the Universe...Thank you for helping me find my match with writing.

Playlist Selects

Here are ten songs from "Can't Match This" playlist!

Feel free to follow the playlist on Spotify to find more songs I felt related to the book.

1. Unpredictable – Jamie Foxx ft Ludacris (R&B)

2. I Don't Want to Be – Gavin DeGaw (Rock)

3. I Need A Girl (Part One) – Diddyft Usher & Loon (Hip-Hop)

4. I'm a Mess – Bebe Rexha (Pop)

5. Doin' What She Likes – Blake Shelton (Country)

6. Chopped N Skrewed – T-Pain ft Ludacris (Rap)

7. Tell Me It's Real – K-Ci & JoJo (R&B)

8. Dreaming of You – Selena (Pop)

9. Closing Time – Semisonic (Rock)

10. U Got It Bad - Usher (R&B)

More songs: https://spoti.fi/2SEDwJi

chapter one

Gideon

"You can't keep leaving me messages like this."

"I can." Lennox, my best friend and biggest pain in my ass, snips. Her face tilts defiantly to the side. "And I most certainly will."

My dark brown eyes widen in annoyance. "This is *ridiculous*." I swiftly lift the note to reiterate my point. "You can't write shit in crayon-"

"Lipstick."

"That's *worse*."

"Is it?"

"Absolutely."

"How do you figure?"

"Because lipstick, even the cheap shit you wear-"

"I don't *wear* cheap shit. I only use it to write with. I *use* the expensive shit you bring me home in those goody bags that you don't want your Insta Ho's to have whenever they give them out at work events."

Her rebuttal receives a frustrated growl.

Lenny simply smirks in return and tucks her long, espresso-colored legs into the leather seat she's occupying.

Why do I do this to myself? Why do I let her suck me into pointless arguments that only end when the thick vein in my forehead is throbbing or my ears are on fire? Why do I continuously subject myself to this shit? Oh, that's right. Because she's my best fucking friend and the only person in the whole goddamn world who could jump off a cliff then somehow convince me I should do it too.

Because there's nothing in this world I wouldn't do for her.

Including whatever bullshit, hair-brained scheme she's about to ask me to do.

I toss the lipstick note, that she left with my secretary this morning when she dropped me off a much needed Cafè Americano, to the side and lean back in my leather office chair. "What is it, Lenny? What's the latest wild hair up your ass convinced you to do?"

"My culo is *not* hairy. I may be lazy about a lot of shit-"

"Such as washing your face in the morning, making *your own* coffee, throwing the breakfast taco bag away-"

"*But*," she emphasizes with a harsh glare, "making sure my body is next to hairless is not one of them."

The imagery forces my face to scrunch for conflicting reasons.

There's the simple fact that's not the kind of shit most people would blurt out to their best friend, particularly if it's a male. Now, once you take into consideration the shit *I've* told *her*, like a cock ring sexcapade gone wrong, her openness seems less abrasive. I shouldn't be blown away by the revelation of her grooming habits. However, as the man who wants to explore every inch of her beautiful, toned body with my tongue, something I've been longing to do since she was a quirky freshman at Clover Rose, the

11

information leak instantly causes my cock to stir. And this is the *real* issue with the depth of our friendship. The line between tappin' ass and comparing gas is paper thin. We spend so much time together it'd be easy to mistake us for a couple, yet we have a tendency to talk like we're just old college pals sharing a few beers. Our private moments consist of sharing bodily functions almost as much as they do snuggling, which is torture when you're madly in love with the person in your arms but can't tell them because you'd rather completely lose the ability to walk than ever risk destroying the friendship you have.

Rock, let me introduce you to the Impossible-to-Penetrate Hard Place.

Lenny uses her index finger to push up her black, box-framed glasses. "You know how I work in the match division of Connect?"

"I know you shouldn't call reading surveys working."

"*Questionnaires.*"

"Potato, potato."

"It's potato, *patata*, asshole."

"Yes. Same shit, different language. Thank you for proving *my* point."

She presses her lips firmly together in obvious irritation.

"Why do you still work there?"

"Because it's *fun.*"

"Setting up socially inept people with sociopaths is fun?"

"Must you belittle my career?"

12

"Career?" I scoff a laugh. "No, being a therapist is a career."

"I'm-"

"On *hiatus*. I know. I'm just saying, *that* is a profession, while this shit is a *hobby* at best."

Her light brown eyes narrow in my direction.

What kind of sane woman walks away from one of the best mental health practices in the state to read third party surveys where she basically just helps people decide who they should be fucking? Money aside, how does it make any sense to go from *actually* helping people to *possibly* helping them? And why?! That's the million-dollar question that burns my brain every time we end up near this subject. I'm Lenny's best fucking friend in the entire world, and I don't know that answer. She tells me everything…except that. It makes me wonder if maybe *she* doesn't even have a clue why she left.

"*Anyway*," she huffs and proceeds to the point, "I've been thinking since I'm great at making matches-"

"Confidence can be crippling."

"-that it's time I find *you* a match."

The end of her sentence receives an eyebrow lift of perplexity.

"Let me find *you* the perfect woman."

I've already found the perfect woman. Fifteen years ago. Problem is, she's completely out of her goddamn mind.

She childishly whines at me. "Come on, Gideon. Please."

"No."

"You never date."

"I'm aware."

"You should be getting laid on the regular."

"I do."

One-night stands are much easier to deal with considering I have yet to discover the best route for falling *out* of love with my best friend. Besides, they fit better into my extensive work schedule, and Lenny-centered hang out routine.

"You really *should* be *dating*, not just fucking whatever underwear model was on the latest cover of *Global Laundry*."

"And you really should be eating more vegetables than the ones you put on tacos."

"Do not drag those demonios into this conversation."

Her hatred of green foods is equal parts fascinating and infuriating.

Heaven fucking forbid they even mention the word salad while we're out at dinner.

"Gideon, you're thirty-five-"

"Which isn't ancient."

"You should be ready to settle *down*. Find the right woman. Start…building your ideal future with her."

The line of remarks reminds me of another woman I'm close to. "Have you been talking to my mother again?"

She tosses a hand nonchalantly in the air. "We met for brunch the other day."

I shut my eyes and shake my head.

My mother...My adorable, meddling mother *insists* I either take the leap and go after Lenny or move on already. While the former is her preference, I've only tried to tip toe down that avenue once in all the years we've been friends, so her faith in me finding the courage to do it again has basically disappeared.

"Come on," she goads, causing me to reopen my eyes. "I do this *professionally*."

"No, you compare idiotic, idealistic ideas from horny people *temporarily*."

"I determine if people are *compatible* and give them the chance to make a connection." Her body shifts around in the seat. "No one knows you better than I do. If anyone can find you your dream woman, it's *me*."

Yup. All she has to do is look in the mirror...

"And regardless of what your misshapen mouth says-"

"It is not misshapen!"

"I know the constant wedding invites from old college pals has begun to bother you..."

They do.

Primarily because I want it to be *our* wedding invites that are going out.

"I know you want what Mick has."

15

I *have* what he has minus the sex. Like what happens between most couples, Minnie, his wife, eventually *became* his best friend. She's always at his side for support. She's always his sounding board of reason, with my opinion, outside of business, coming in second now, as it should in a marriage. They hang out. They go out. They laugh, fight, and annoy each other. They share everything just like me and Lennox.

Well.

Almost everything.

"Let me find you love."

Gagging can't be helped.

"At least give me a *shot*."

My fingers fold tightly together in my lap.

Maybe now would be the ideal time to tell her. Maybe I could say, "It's an impossible task because the only woman I wanna spend the rest of my life with is *you*." Then maybe she'll gasp, bounce out of her seat, and drop into my lap.

Yeah.

That thought is as ridiculous as the contract negotiation I'm currently working on for Drake Lenzi to endorse this brand of foreign watches.

"What's in it for me?"

"*Love.*"

I wave my hand around to brush off the notion.

"Fine." Lenny rolls her eyes. "What do you want?"

16

It only takes a moment for my mind to settle on something obvious and beneficial. "If you *don't* manage to find me...a *match-*"

"*Love.*"

"You're not going to find me love, Lenny. The best you'll probably come across is a woman I want a second date with."

Still *highly* unlikely.

"Now, when you don't-"

"*If.*"

"-you'll quit Connect and take a job offer as a therapist at this practice that focuses on mentally preparing athletes from their transition out of majors into retirement."

"I'd rather eat an entire bag of lima beans."

"And I'd rather continue to dip my dick in the shallow waters of detachment."

Lying.

Much rather dive between her tight thighs and set up shop for a lifetime.

Her index finger flies to her teeth to endure a nibbling.

An adorable, self-destructive habit.

"You knew I wasn't going to even *consider* this idea without some sort of negotiation in place." A smug smile slips onto my face. "Negotiating is what I do, Lenny. Day in and day out."

Just typically for athletes and not to maintain my status as a single man.

She chews harder.

"What's the big deal?" I playfully poke. "You're *great* at matchmaking, remember?"

"You're an asshole."

"Your favorite one."

Lenny rolls her eyes once more, although this one is alongside a smile. "How many dates do I get?"

"Three."

"Fuck that. *Ten.*"

"Fuck *that*. Five."

"Siete."

The number sounds doable; however, I don't immediately concede. All the best agents know you never immediately agree on the change even when it's the one you can live with. You let the other party sit. Simmer. Stew. Sometimes you get a better offer that way. Unfortunately, that's not the case with Lenny. She's equally as stubborn as I am.

"Seven dates to find me a woman that I want a *second* date with. And when you fail-"

"*If.*"

"-then you take the job."

"And when I succeed-"

18

"*Impossible-*"

"You make *me* best man in your wedding."

She can't be the best man *and* the bride.

I bite my tongue to stop the rebuttal from escaping. "You have a deal."

"Put it in writing."

A teasing grin grows on my face. "Should I use the same shade you did, or maybe something a little more summery?"

Lenny lets her head fall back on a body shaking laugh.

While I lightly chuckle, I let my eyes devour the age-old sight.

She's naturally stunning. From her head full of curls she has trouble taming, to the shapely figure she hides with gym clothes, she is undoubtedly perfect. There isn't an inch of her brown skin that I've seen that I don't love. I know the distinct beauty marks like the dark freckle near her mouth and the three that surround her right knee. I know the scars that usually stay hidden, such as the one on her foot that's from shattering a glass jar of salsa when she was thirteen. I even know the slight difference in the way her body curves during a month where she's on the wagon of working out versus the way it's a little extra cushiony when hot wings are winning. Over the years, I have studied everything about Lenny like an NFL contract I can't seem to close.

She'll never find me someone unless she realizes my perfect match is *her*.

And if she hasn't come to that conclusion by now...Will she ever?

chapter two

Lennox

She extends her purple plastic fork in my direction. "Bite, Auntie Len Len."

I know it would be wrong to tell her to get that weak shit out of here...I mean, she's only two. She doesn't completely understand what she's being brainwashed into eating. Who am I to destroy her confidence over one of the only decisions she's capable of making or the nutritional bond her mother has established.

It's not my place.

Just like it's not hers to try to poison me with green beans.

The only way Lennox Marston will experience death by food will be from a hot wings challenge that gets the best of me.

And at this point, it's *highly unlikely*. I've beaten each one I've come across. My mouth tolerance for spicy foods is ridiculous. Gideon loves to joke how he'd sign me up for the Food Olympics if there was one.

Jaye Cox, one of the only female friends I have, intervenes with a smile. "No, no, Rainne. Those are *your* veggies. They're for *you* to eat."

Rainne scrunches her light cappuccino complexion in objection.

Ah.

Now I see.

She doesn't like them either and wanted someone else to suffer as well.

Rude.

Rude toddler.

Jaye strolls over to the table, caressing her swollen stomach along the way. "Two more bites of your green beans, and then we can watch *Boss Baby*."

"*Boss Baby*!" Rainne repeats with glee.

"What the hell is that?" Carly Chambers, one of Jaye's friends who is starting to become one of mine through association, quickly questions.

Our friend takes the utensil from her daughter's clutches, stabs one of the green beans, and offers it to her child. "Are you serious? You've never heard of *Boss Baby*?"

"Why would I have heard of that?" Carly counters. "I don't have *kids* or nieces…though Dusty has two, so there's a good chance someday I will technically have two, too…" Her voice begins to drift away in a longing fashion, but she swiftly shakes it away. "Anyway, what is it? Like a game show or something?"

Bewilderment bulldozes its way onto Jaye's coffee shaded face. "You really think they make *game shows* for kids?"

"Uh…yeah!" I interject with enthusiasm. "Throw it back to the '90s for the *best* examples. *Guts. Legends of the Hidden Temple. Double Dare. Family Double Dare. Wild-*"

"Point proven," Jaye declares as she feeds Rainne one more bite of vegetables.

"Effortlessly," Carly compliments.

My grin grows, and I tuck both my feet into the wooden chair to rest my head on top of my bent knees.

"*Boss Baby* is a show based on the *movie Boss Baby*. Basically, small children getting into shenanigans."

"*Rugrats* rip off," I loudly mumble.

"Don't start that again," Jaye scolds at the same time she removes Rainne from her booster seat.

"Wasn't that *also* a show from the '90s?"

My smirk returns. "It was."

"Are you like a '90s Trivia expert or something?"

"Is that a job?" I cock a curious eyebrow. "Because I would take it without any care or concern to how much it paid."

Which is more or less the situation I'm already in. Working at Connect was not something I ever saw myself doing, but then again, there isn't exactly *much* I really see myself doing. My parents think I lack direction. My siblings think I lack drive. My best friend is convinced I lack discipline. Truthfully? I just don't understand the point of mundaneness. Why wake up every day and not experience *more* of life? Why sit in an office sixty hours a week being paid hundreds of thousands of dollars you're never gonna get to spend? Why waste your life conforming to what society tells you to rather than living an adventure?

And I believe my adventure is incredible despite what others have to say about it.

They're the ones moaning and groaning about never getting a break to just watch an episode of whatever reality music competition show they're into now, while I'm the one out here seeing famous actors do impromptu karaoke at dive bars. Gideon and I *still* talk about witnessing Levi Stone sing his heart out anytime his face appears on the T.V.

We've had a lot of great moments over the years...

Ah, who am I kidding?

All our moments together are great.

That's just how it is when you're spending time with the person you love most in the world.

Jaye takes just a moment to set up Rainne on the couch with her favorite show.

They really are an adorable little family, and Rainne takes after both her parents. While she has Jaye's toffee eyes, brown skin, and bouncy curls, she has Archer's thinner nose, higher cheek bones, and constantly calloused hands from playing too rough. Personality-wise she pulls traits from both of them the same way most toddlers do.

When Jaye finally waddles back into the kitchen, she's clearly displaying more discomfort than before.

"Sit," I sweetly insist seconds prior to serenading her with the opening to the chorus of "Just Kickin' It" by Xscape.

"Didn't that song *also* come out in the '90s?" Carly promptly inquires.

My wink is exaggerated.

Jaye giggles and strokes her stomach gently. "I don't remember being this exhausted with Rainne."

"You weren't, but then again, you didn't have a toddler to chase around in between working and being a wife." The reminder is proceeded with me adding, "I don't know how you do it."

"Ditto," Carly chimes in.

"Do either of you have *interest* in some day learning the ancient secrets of the working mom?"

Her hinting at our thoughts on a family force my attention elsewhere.

Oh…the F word I'm *least* fond of.

It's not that I don't like families. Considering most of the counseling I do and have done is in regard to relationships, particularly that of marriage and family, it would be fair to say I *love* families. The dynamics. The blending of backgrounds. The miniature societies they often become. It's fascinating and fun! Hell, my own oversized family, is a ball of chaos I love being around. However, the F word immediately becomes a burden when your own has recently started riding you about when you're going to contribute to its growth and that your eggs are not indeed little humans for you to possibly hatch when *you're ready,* so much as goods with expiration dates waiting to be baked. My mother nagged me on and off about getting married and giving her grandbabies the later part of my twenties. Now that I'm in my thirties? That shit feels like a pre-recorded message I am played back each week when I make the mistake of answering her calls instead of my dad's.

Carly doesn't verbally answer. There's no real need to. By the brightness of her beaming, it's easy to guess she's already given her fictional children names.

Sometimes I do the same. They're mostly English-Spanish fusions I know would get butchered by just about everyone outside of me and my future baby daddy.

25

My cellphone vibrates on the table in front of me, and I reach out to check the notification.

Seeing a text from Gideon immediately instills a smile on my face.

OG: Strip?

Me: In mixed company?

I snicker to myself at the comeback knowing the frown it's receiving.

OG: Wanna cook for yourself?

Me: Crab Cake.

OG: Making requests or calling me names?

Another small giggle escapes.

"Must be Gideon," Jaye slyly comments. "The only person you laugh like that for."

I cut her a brief glance. "Not true."

"Very true."

My fingers hastily fly across the keys to reply.

Me: Get Ribeyes. I'll bring beer.

OG: Runt's.

Me: I am full-sized sir!

OG: * this is where you insert an eye roll from me Lenny *

I chuckle, toss my phone back on the table, and gnaw on the nail of my index finger.

"Lennox, when are you gonna stop pretending you're not in love with your best friend and just go after him?" Jaye brashly asks. "It's not like it isn't *super* obvious to anyone with eyes and ears."

"Well, doesn't pregnancy make you bold," Carly playfully taunts, wagging her chocolate colored finger in our best friend's direction.

"Blunt," Jaye heavily sighs. "*Too* blunt for my own good sometimes. Last week, I told Archer there were other seasonings in the cabinet, and it would be okay if he used them occasionally."

"Damn…" My stretched-out version of the word causes her shoulders to slump more.

"I don't mean to come off bitchy. I really don't. I mean I really *really* don't. That's not the kind of person I am. You all know that's not *me*. The real me. The me who tried eight different pies last year at the police family cookout and pretended they were all amazing so I didn't hurt anyone's feelings. But for some reason this baby…" She gently pats her tummy. "He's…wreaking a different kind of havoc than Rainne did."

"I'll say." My chime in receives their attention. "With Rainne you were like sunshine and slurpies, but with him you're balled fists and burgers."

Jaye hums to herself. "Great. Now I want a hamburger."

"Want me to text Archer so you don't have to get your phone?" Carly volunteers.

"Please...Hopefully he'll read the text before the sun fucking sets." Her attention jerks back to me expecting an answer. "Well?"

"Well, what?"

"Well, when are you going to finally breakdown and confess to him you've been in love with him for like...fifteen years?"

I chew harder on the side of my nail.

It hasn't been the *whole* fifteen years. That would be...*insane*. It's only been more like fourteen and some change. After all, it wasn't love at first sight. Or it could've been... I don't really know. I was drunk. And dancing. And then barfing. There wasn't really time to have a deep, meaningful connection, though offering to help me wash the vomit out of my hair was a sweet gesture. Gotta admit. I don't know any other guys who would've offered to give a chick a salon style scrub in their kitchen sink at three a.m.

"You're in love with your best friend? That's so cute," Carly coos.

"It's not *cute*," I chomp. "And it's not *true*."

Because in order for shit to be true you have to admit it to someone other than yourself between bowls of salsa and sports highlights on ESPN.

Jaye rolls her eyes in objection. "Very true."

My huff is louder than before. "If it were true then I wouldn't be setting him up on dates!"

"What?!" The two of them question in tandem.

"Gideon agreed to let me set him up on a few dates. I created him the perfect profile and have been handling all of his match

28

choices *personally*, which is my job *anyway*, but I'm giving the women I think would be a good fit for him an extra thorough check."

You know, weighing how obnoxious I may find them in the long run versus how easy they may be to get along with in the short one. That and, of course, finding a female who is *nothing* like me because he already has me. He doesn't need another. There can't be two of us! Only one Highlander!

"Everything you're saying sounds horrible," Jaye callously states.

"How many dates?" Carly questions.

"Seven. Seven chances to find him love…"

Feels like the least I can do since it'll never be me he sees that way.

"Or more accurately, seven chances to find him a woman he wants to go on a second date with."

"And what happens if you don't in that time frame?" Carly continues to engage in the conversation.

"I…have to take a stupid job I don't want." My shoulder shrug is simple. "No biggie."

"Because why would changing careers *be* a big deal?" Carly sarcastically retorts.

"It's *less* of a big deal when it's just her going back to what she used to do and *still* does now, though only in a volunteer capacity."

Parke's Place is a Military Vet Shelter where I counsel in my non-match making hours. Back in college at Clover Rose, I accrued my clinical training hours in a similar setting. I enjoyed working with veterans, helping them, as well as their loved ones, through the difficult transition from active solider to civilian. Nowadays, I spend my time helping *couples* through hardships they weren't expecting to endure or have trouble understanding. The men and women who seek my advice are dealing with various issues, such as PTSD and how it is affecting their family, whether it's them starting one or perhaps rocking one that's already established. My door is open to *any* individual who once served our country. It's a non-charity organization that pays me for the few hours a week I provide my time, but the money is not enough to live off of. Otherwise I would…Without question. Helping others is probably my favorite part of life's adventure right next to watching basketball with Gideon and eating tacos at midnight. I met Archer and Jaye a few years back through a couple's counseling session I used to host. Once I became the primary in-house counselor for the shelter, I had to abandon the group sessions but kept in touch with them. Before I knew it, we were becoming friends. And now…basically best friends.

"Okay, let's rewind," Carly casually requests, hand movements mocking her words. "Do you actually have feelings for this guy?"

My silence is my admission.

She nods slowly. "And…do you think there's any chance…I mean *any chance* he might be a tiny bit remotely interested in you?"

"Yes!" Jaye squeaks. "A thousand times yes!"

"Too loud, Mommy," Rainne whines from the other room.

I point a finger at her. "I agree with the tot."

Jaye shoots daggers in my direction before selling me down the river. "Lennox is the only person incapable of seeing the truth."

My brown eyes roll of their own accord.

30

"She has this whole bullshit theory-"

"It's a good theory!"

"-that she uses to keep herself from becoming vulnerable, which as a licensed psychologist who went to school for almost a decade, she should be able to recognize as her own self constricting behavior."

I can.

And I do.

And I *choose* to ignore it.

Much like my doctor's suggestion that I eat less refried beans and more of the ones my little honorary niece tried to feed me earlier.

Carly crosses her legs and folds her hands on top of her knee. "Tell me this theory."

"It's simple." Sitting completely up, I nonchalantly explain, "I'm the bro', not the ho'."

An unimpressed expression crosses Carly's face.

"Basically, I'm *not* that chick. I'm the one you guzzle beer with while shouting at football games, not sip martinis with at the Mayor's Ball. I'm the one you burp the alphabet against, not the one you rush to the bathroom just to fart for. I'm the one you call when you've got this weird bump on your balls and your Google search makes you feel like what you thought was an ingrown hair is now a new form of cancer."

"That's...oddly *specific*," Jaye mutters.

"Mick flips out at basically *any* body abnormality and considering the fact his wife looks like she was edited in PicMonkey, he has a tendency to call me."

"And who is Mick?" Carly asks.

"My other best guy friend. Him and Gideon were roommates all throughout college and a couple years after it too. They actually started a sport's agency together. A+ Athletes. Currently ranked the best agency in the state and like fourth best in the entire country, though if you're talking to either of them, they'll swear they're third."

Carly nods her understanding.

Mick and Gideon are physically opposite, yet mentally compatible. Mick is blonde, blue-eyed, and shaped like he's promoting a diet pill for men, while Gideon is brunette, brown-eyed, and built like the professional fullback he was at one point hellbent on becoming. What they differ for in form, they over compensate in brotherhood. They're practically into the same types of women, same types of expensive food, and same types of sports. It's one of those things that make them great business partners.

"Anyway, you get the picture. I'm not *that* woman. I'm not the one you spend weeks ring shopping for or plan some ludicrous proposal that most likely involves sky writing. I'm not someone you call your fiancée and take home to meet tu madre, though I would have no problem taking whiskey or bourbon shots with tu padre."

More confusion appears in Carly's eyes. "Wait, you speak *Spanish*?"

"Mmm…Occasionally. I have a tendency to mix and match my languages when I'm really tired, flustered, or excited."

"Talking *about* and *to* Gideon has a tendency to make her *all* of those things."

I send a sneer Jaye's direction.

My little unborn nephew is turning her into Sabrina The Teenage Witch's long lost, wicked aunt.

"The point I'm trying to make is, I'm the best friend *not* the booty."

"Let me start by saying that was all elegantly put," Carly chuckles, "but as someone who also deals with relationships daily, can I make a suggestion in your latest matchmaking endeavor?"

"Sure."

"Put yourself on the list."

To think I was gonna praise her for being supportive when Jaye wasn't…

"Put yourself on the list as number six."

"Why?"

"Friends to lovers is a much more missed scenario than people realize when searching for someone to spend their life with. People, women especially, tend to look over the male figure who is already in their life because in their own mind they have decided if the man wanted them, he would've done something about it already. Sometimes, this *is* the case. Other times, men need a big red arrow pointing them in the right direction. Tell me, when you're talking to couples, who has a more difficult time communicating and opening up in most cases?"

There's no hesitation in my response. "Men."

33

"Exactly. So…there's a possibility…Gideon struggles with that ability himself. If you slyly place yourself on the list, or hell, slyly place yourself more directly in his line of vision as a viable match, you give him the chance to see what it is that maybe he's been too blind to see."

Her logic sends my finger back to my teeth.

"Or, if you're *not* his match, it also gives you both the moment of insight to come to that conclusion as well."

"Why can't she just go first then?" Jaye promptly asks.

"It's a process," Carly clarifies. "She can't go first because he might brush it off as a bad joke, but she can't go last for the same reason. She has to put herself between other *real* possibilities to prove the point."

Damn her.

That's *brilliant*.

And a much safer way to sample the relationship salsa.

"On a *different* note," Carly's brown stare soars back to me, "if you don't lose this…bet…?"

"Deal."

"Okay. If you don't lose this deal and want to give up reading surveys to help couples, let me know. I work for the same company that owns Connect except on the personal matchmaking side that deals with more exclusive clientele. We're looking to expand the services we provide to include relationship counseling. Basically, you'd be giving advice to newly matched couples, couples who have used our services in the past but are having troubles, and even some of our success stories who may seek advice for maintaining their happy marriage."

34

The offer receives an interested hum. "You should pitch the idea for a private ask for advice site or chat line. That way if they are too intimidated to come in or don't have time or maybe are out of the state and need help, they can receive it."

Carly's eyebrows lunge upward in surprise. "That's a *really* good idea."

"I know. I'm very wise," I jokingly state.

The three of us share in a round of laughter though the job suggestion lingers in the front of my mind.

Helping couples is my jam. It's why I thought connecting people through this dating website would be fun. There's something about the fusing of two individuals that I find intoxicating...Absolutely, totally, Cher from *Clueless* level of magical. That moment where she sets up her teachers is one I still hold close to my heart. It's the pure euphoria in indulging in *others'* joy. I get that from counseling too. Knowing you're helping people heal what was once a wonderful partnership is the gift that keeps on giving. You're making *their* adventure through time a little easier or a little more worthwhile by giving them back something they thought was lost.

Truthfully? I *have* that relationship with Gideon...

Sure, we don't grope each other in the front seat of his Lambo or sneak off to bone in the bathroom stall of a business function, but we basically have everything else.

That should be enough. I've always *made* it enough. I figure, every day he sticks by me through another round of crazy is a miracle I don't take for granted.

Maybe that's why I've never let myself be open to more.

You have to risk what you have in order to possibly gain something greater.

I'm not sure I can do that.

Definitely not now.

Not with the career sting slightly still lingering.

Not while we operate our lifestyles in opposite fashions.

Not when there's an actual opportunity for him to find a more suitable match.

Huh.

Why do I get the feeling there will never be a good time to take such a risk?

chapter three

Gideon

His jaw drops at the same time he frantically points to the contract in front of him. "You're serious?"

"Yes."

"This isn't a prank?"

"Do I look like I have the time to create elaborate jokes?"

Shemar Morris, easily the most beloved and praised player on the Highland Hellcats basketball team, slowly starts to smile in disbelief. "This is...*insane*."

"This is my job," I remind him while adjusting my black tie.

An almost goofy grin grows on his brown-skinned face. "I can't believe it..." He thrusts himself backwards into the leather office chair he's occupying. "Hell, I can hardly believe any of the shit that's been happening over the past three years." His brown eyes flood with gratitude. "Working with you has changed my entire fucking career."

Changed...*Launched*. Same shit.

His agent before me was a joke at best. Even in my earlier years, I pulled better clients than he ever did. Since switching to me, we got him off that shitty west coast team, an increase in salary, party invitations from actual princesses, and endorsement deals he can literally do in his sleep. The thing I find most interesting about all of it is the fact his *ego* hasn't caught up to his new status. Shemar still behaves like the humble, hill country-raised kid he was afraid no one in the league would ever take seriously.

He reminds me of Lenny that way.

Regardless of the degrees, which she refuses to hang on her wall because they would distract from her out of date music posters, the papers she's published in numerous journals —though Lenny pretends she doesn't read them, and six figures that would be something to brag about in her field, she maintains her down to earth, '90s addicted, salsa must be eaten with tacos roots.

I'm thankful for it.

I've changed enough for the both of us.

"Okay," Shemar starts to nod, "explain one more time what it is I have to do."

"Simple. We sign the deal, and you become a 'social' endorser."

"Which means what?"

"You post about these shoes on social media weekly, which I negotiated it down from daily emphasizing it would be *overkill* and more likely to harm the brand than to help it. You wear them to social functions that would allow this type of footwear. You encourage your fans, friends, and family to share or reshare the *positive* promotion you're posting. *Most* importantly, you wear these to practice...*every practice*. Now, they're not league regulation, however, Big L is one of the men who *owns* your team, so it would be wise if he got wind to you wearing his product while working for him." There's no time for him to cogitate my explanation. I place my black fountain pen down directly on top of the contract with one hand and use the other to ring my secretary. "Sign."

"This is Kristen," she answers cheerfully.

"Bring Shemar his bag of cherry sours and me my schedule."

"Coming."

The call ends, and Shemar pushes the completed contract my way. "You wine and dine all your players?"

"I do." Kristen opens the door with the requested items in hand. "Unfortunately, not everyone is as easy going as you." I motion her in with two fingers. "Enjoy your treat. A rep from their company will reach out to one of yours by the end of the week."

Shemar offers me one last smile, stands, and smoothly shifts the bag of candy from Kristen's hands to his.

The "treats" for meetings was a late-night idea Lenny gave me the balls to implement. Around midnight, probably the most magical hour of our friendship, we were finishing off a pizza when the idea hit me. Business is not only about being *better* than the competitor but being *remembered* as being better. The more you can stand out...the more you can leave an impression, the more likely you are to capture the client. Mick and I were still in the early days of launching the company, and Lenny was right there with us, delivering late night dinners or shots of espresso. That night, I threw out the idea of giving personalized five-star treatment to *every player* I signed. Of course, other agencies did shit like give you a glass of champagne or the perfect coffee order, but the notion of taking it a step further kept gnawing at me until I verbalized it to my other half.

Better half.

Fuck.

Not the point.

Lenny told me to go for it but be careful because superficial appreciation of a person always backfires. So, I put the extra time in.

39

Researched their favorites in the beginning before wising up and having them fill out a survey upon signing. The business grew, however, the practice is still in place. We now have the paperwork in their files, as well as have our clients resubmit the form each time they resign with us.

It's one of the little things that helps keep A+ Athletes best in the state and third in the country.

Once he's out of ear shot, I reach for my cellphone and request information, "Schedule."

"Phone call with Combs in fifteen minutes. He wants to discuss a potential restaurant deal."

"He *always* wants to discuss a potential restaurant deal."

"Video conference with Rice who wants his salary with the Highflyers renegotiated for next season-"

"*This* season's not even over yet."

"You have a two o'clock face-to-face with Crosby to discuss this quarter's finances."

My groan is glued to my aggressive scrolling over emails I do not intend to open this morning.

This is the drawback to being licensed to work with clients in more than one league. The work pile is endless.

"And you have a five o'clock appointment with Shalinda."

"Cancel."

"You can't cancel."

I grunt when I finally reach the end of unopened mail. "I *can*. And I *am*."

"You can't cancel, sir."

Tossing my phone to the side, I divert my stare to the adorable, petite blonde who rarely gives me any sort of pushback.

Lenny begged me to hire her, though made me promise I wouldn't fuck her.

Sometimes I wonder if that was because *she* wanted me or just didn't want me to ruin things with the one other woman outside my mother and Minnie that she trusts.

"You made me *swear* to not let you cancel."

My hand motion dismisses her statement.

"You also made me *swear* to not come in for a whole week if you refused to take me seriously."

Why is past me such an insistent asshole?

"It's *just* a haircut, Kristen."

"Hair and face."

I give the thick scruff on my jaw a casual stroke. "Semantics."

She hums and types something on her tablet. Afterward, she turns it around to face me and hits play.

A video recording of what is obviously me last week begins to scold. "Get. Your. Fucking. Hair. Cut. You're starting to look like Tom Hardy in *Mad Max*."

"That's not a bad look."

"It *is* when you're planning to close a multimillion-dollar contract between a Superbowl champion and the biggest whiskey company in the country."

Fair point.

The video ends, and my eyes relocate to Kristen's smug smirk. "Fine. *Keep* the appointment."

She notes something on her tablet before informing, "Lennox left you a note on her way to work. Would you like it now?"

"Why didn't she just text me?"

"She said her phone was dead-"

"I *just* bought her a new wireless charger. She can *literally* leave the damn thing just sitting there without having to search for a cord or a free outlet."

"Which she said you would probably point out and wanted me to say..." Her teeth briefly bite into her bright red stained lips. "'Stop buying me expensive shit you know I'll lose'."

Huh.

Even *less* surprised she's prepared to argue with me than I am with myself.

"Would you like the note?"

"Yes."

Kristen bounces out of the room, passing by Mick who is entering.

Unlike most men who can't keep their dick down when catching sight of my assistant, he barely acknowledges her presence. Hard to blame him considering the woman he's married to is the literal definition of a blonde bombshell. Her name pays a beautiful homage to her waistline yet not much else. Most of her is natural, but she's begun the long and tricky game of casually nipping and tucking to keep up with her competition in the fashion world. She's a stylist who has to look red carpet ready despite the fact she rarely walks it. Paired with Mick, they have the look of Hollywood royalty, which is an impression he finds important to maintain.

I don't.

Yeah, I'll smile for the photos and clink glasses while laughing at a joke that isn't funny no matter how many shots you've had, but I refuse to force myself into a relationship with someone for the simple status benefits it may throw me.

Not to say that's *why* Mick and Minnie are together...However, I can say, it definitely weighed in their decisions to continue dating during the beginning of their relationship.

Business is the harshest sport of them all.

The season never ends.

The players get traded without consent.

Salary can fluctuate in spite of your best performance and image is often more important than your actual skills.

"Got a minute?" He questions, hands finding their way to his black suit pockets.

"Probably."

Kristen returns and places a crumbled receipt in front of me.

43

My disapproving look is instant. "Are you fucking kidding me?"

"She refused to rewrite the message on a sticky note. I *tried*."

Mick lightly chuckles. "That from Lennox?"

"Do you know anyone else who would leave one of the top sport's agents in the country a memo on the back of a receipt for tacos?"

"How do you know it's tacos?" Kristen quickly questions.

In unison, Mick and I reply, "It's *always* tacos."

I drop my attention down to the words scribbled in neon blue Sharpie.

Woman can find that no problem but not a pen?

Date # 1: Coffee @ Loca Mocha Casabloca @ Noon. Blonde. Kindergarten Teacher. Bekka.

"Why didn't she just email me this?"

"And just how many emails have you checked today?" Mick playfully pokes.

"None of them are urgent. I checked." Kristen giggles at the retort, reminding me she can be dismissed. "That'll be all. Thank you."

She promptly exits, making sure to shut the door behind her.

Mick tosses a nod towards the note. "Is it important?"

"Not really."

44

"What is it?"

"A date."

"With Lennox?"

I have to stop myself from adding the words unfortunately not to the conversation. "*From* Lenny."

Confusion carves its way onto his expression.

"I agreed to let her set me up on a few dates."

"Why?"

"For her own good."

Disarray remains in his stare.

"We negotiated a deal last week-"

"As one does with their best friend."

"-in which she has seven dates to find a woman I want to go out with more than once or she has to give up this ridiculous after school job and take the *adult* one where she can actually *help* people rather than just intervene like a scene from her favorite movie."

"Which is…?"

"*Clueless.*"

Though she read the Jane Austen novel it was loosely based on and was not *nearly* as interested.

Took her three weeks and a promise to treat her to Lupe Del Rio for her to finish.

Mick shakes off the information. "And *why* does she suddenly wanna hook you up?"

"My guess is because she needs something more meaningful to do than what she's doing day to day. Or it could be that she has this hole inside of her she wants to fill with full time counseling at the shelter but can't because they'll never be able to pay her enough to live off of. Then again, perhaps the random idea was spawned thanks to a brunch she had with my mother who more than likely bullied her into bullying me into doing more than banging Instagram models and flight attendants." An innocent shrug bounces my shoulders. "Regardless of the reason, I agreed to prove to her I'm *right* about this matchmaking shit being a terrible impulsive decision that is time to move past."

"Or…instead of playing bullshit mind games with her, you could just *go* for it."

I don't respond.

"Perhaps finally confess how you've wanted her since we were juniors in college, and you saw her shamelessly do the Hammer Time dance in the middle of a frat party."

It was equal parts impressive and embarrassing for both of us. No chick should *ever* bust out the moves to a '90s classic in a room full of men she's hoping wanna bang her, and no dude should ever wanna bang a chick who appears as if she studied the music video like a how-to manual, yet I did *want* to…She was vibrant. And carefree. And unapologetically herself rather than who everyone else wanted her to be. She was a freshman in college so that shit was profound, especially when all the females who were constantly on my jock at that point were busy *pretending* to be whoever it was they thought they needed to be to ride my dick. I watched her dance her ass off while rapping along, blaming the fact I knew all the words on the beer in my system.

46

It was a lie.

I fucking love that song.

We fucking love that song to this day.

Plays every time we're in my car together.

Every. Time.

"Let me give you some advice," Mick obnoxiously begins.

"Is it the same advice you've been brow beating me to death with for the past fifteen years."

"Ten."

"Thirteen."

"Twelve," he counters one final time, "but yes. It's the same fucking advice because, obviously, you are walking proof of repetition being necessary for the human brain to make life sustaining changes."

My eyes soar to the ceiling.

"The next time Lennox leaves that boyfriend door cracked, you need to kick that shit in like the Kool-Aid man."

I toss him a sardonic stare. "He barged in through the wall."

"Even. Better."

Feeling my irritation grow on a subject I already hate over analyzing, I throw a hand in the air in question. "What did you *actually* need?"

"I bought us tickets to a charity function next month."

47

"What else is new?"

"*Date* required."

"Then I won't go."

"*Not* an option."

"Not attending is always an option."

"Not when we both need to be there to impress the father of a fifteen-year-old hockey player."

The disinterested expression on my face remains.

"I've seen the kid play, Gideon. He's got pro potential right out of the gate. We could sign him up. Steer him. Launch his career into the hall of fame by the time he's twenty-five."

I drum my fingers against the top of my wooden desk.

"We *need* more NHL players. We rep three right now."

"We don't *need* more of anything, Mick."

He frowns at the rebuttal.

"Between me and Simmons alone, we have hands in every major sports league...*including* CFL, which is a notable mention when you take into consideration there are only *nine* teams."

A small smirk threatens his face.

"Once you add in the other agents, we could collectively put together a whole team in most of those major league divisions and maybe one or two in the minors. We're doing phenomenal right now."

"We can always do better." He tilts his head condescendingly at me. "Like two spots better."

"You wanna be number one in the nation."

"Don't you?"

I wanna work *less* and drink beer *more*. Although I hate Lenny's flaky behavior where her job is concerned, it's almost admirable. For her, happiness always wins over a paycheck. She'd rather live life eating frozen burritos every night for dinner than be chained to a career she considers a chore. It's one of those things I need her in my life for. She forces me to come up for air, while I remind her of the importance of letting her feet occasionally touch the ground.

"Be there," Mick commands as he begins to back out of my office. "Bring Lennox."

The wink he shoots me receives my middle finger.

Knowing me, I probably will. Anytime there is someone I *need* to impress versus someone I just have to tolerate, I take her. She can talk about the business and sports with the best of us. Hell, if she had any interest in really switching careers instead of just pretending, I'd hire her in a heartbeat. She's not great with numbers or organization, but those are skills that can be *taught*. A passion for something can't.

I'd know.

I tried to let the one I have for football go after it turned its back on me.

Couldn't do it.

Kinda like my unresolved feelings for Lenny.

49

**

Walking into the popular local coffee shop, I immediately survey the scene in hopes the woman hasn't arrived yet. Like always, the place is packed from wall to wall with various types of people. The line itself is being occupied by what appears to be a local college student, a biker, a business man, and a couple that can't seem to untangle their tongues long enough to move forward. Just as I prepare to slip into it, I notice a woman in the corner, near the side front window, eagerly trying to peer around people to get a view of the door.

Is that her?

Why couldn't Lenny have texted me her photo?

Oh…that's right. Because she is incapable of keeping her phone charged.

And when I make this argument to her later how asinine that is, she's going to counter with, why couldn't I have just checked the email account she created specifically for this dating debacle. The answer to that is simple of course. Because I don't *want* to engage with any of these women more than I have to.

I carefully begin to inch toward her, finding myself more and more impressed with each step I take.

If that is her, which would only prove how well Lenny really does know me, then from looks alone we're off to a good start.

Long, blonde hair…not a necessity but an increasing favorite. Big doe eyes screaming her innocence. Slender, fit frame that was most likely accomplished via a weekly yoga or spin class. Clothing tight enough to display her B-cup chest that is trying to pass for a C due to the hardworking push up bra underneath.

As fucked up as it is, I prefer to have my one offs with women who look nothing like the one I don't have the balls to invite into my bed. Lenny isn't anywhere *near* model perfect nor does she care. She has tight brown curls that are the boss of her most days, beautiful brown eyes that are magnified by glasses she refuses to ditch, and a body that she only works out during our random athletic spurts like playing basketball on the court in my backyard or doing the forgotten, but once very popular, Tae Bo videos.

I wonder if my constant choice in the same type of fuck buddies keeps her from seeing my attraction to *her*.

"Gideon?!" The blonde squeaks, voice similar to something from a 1930's Disney movie.

Hiding my repulsion to the sound is difficult. "Bekka with two Ks?"

"That's me!" She pops up onto her feet and promptly extends her manicured hand. During our shaking, she adds, "I look just like my picture, right?!"

"Right."

Probably?

"Thank Heavens, you look *just* like your picture too. I was worried I was getting cat lynched."

Certain I misheard her, I question, "Cat…lynched?"

"You know, where someone posts a fake photo then you meet them and they're like a whole other person."

"*Catphished.*"

"You know, I'm really not into seafood..." She shrugs off the correction. "Probably why I used the less popular term."

Not a term used at all.

"Fish really are meant to be our friends. We need to love our oceans more. That's definitely what the Aquaman movie taught me."

"Okay." I clear my throat to rid the urge of saying a snarky comment. "I'm gonna order myself a cup of coffee. Would you like anything?"

"Goodie doodles here," Bekka announces at the same time she points to the cup on the table.

She's given a short nod of acknowledgment before I turn to begin my stroll back to the line.

Almost immediately, she offers, "Do you wanna sit while I grab it?"

I give my teeth a silent, brief suck and toss her the kindest smile I can. "No thanks. I've got it."

"You sure?"

"Positive."

Her tiny lips curl into a pout, but she plops back down into her seat.

This is the problem with having a permanent limp. It always shifts people's perspectives of you. Regardless of your status or what you're clearly capable of, they have a tendency to view you as weak or an invalid. They wanna rescue you despite the fact you don't *need* rescuing. Just because I have a physical flaw doesn't mean I'm helpless.

52

Once I've ordered and retrieved my beverage, I weave my way around the crowd to return to our table.

Bekka doesn't bother waiting for me to settle into my seat. "Did you get an ouchy earlier today? Maybe pulling a muscle at the gym?" Her eyes do a quick sweep of my business attire covered frame. "You're in *amazing* shape…" She lets her stare stroke my broad shoulders and bulging biceps that are being contained by a navy-blue button up. "Like *gold star* amazing."

Her continuous child friendly word choices must be a direct reflection of her career…

Or at least that's what I'm going to assume.

Or more accurately *hope*.

I adjust my tie and smile at the compliment. "Thank you."

"So, is that it?" Bekka inquires. "Is that why you're limping?"

"No. It's a permanent limp."

"Permanent as in you'll always have it?"

Literal definition.

Opting for less sarcasm strains my neck muscles. "That's what the doctors say."

An intrigued expression I do not approve of appears on her face. "Huh…How'd you get it? Were you like…born with a boo boo?"

53

"No." Resisting the instinct to let my eye twitch at her vocabulary increases exponentially. "I was a fullback in college and got severely injured during a game."

"What do you mean severely injured?"

"Fractured pelvis. Broken leg in multiple places. And testicular trauma."

Her tiny hands fly dramatically to her cheeks.

"Oh my stars!"

Really?

She can't even *cuss* properly?

"The...injury is what shifted me from the pro career I was headed towards to legally representing pros in their careers."

Lenny and Mick were the only people who didn't abandon me throughout the incident. They were both at my side. Supported me through therapy. Through the fake sympathy. Through the shunning. As if it were *my fault*. As if I tackled myself. As if I wanted to spend the rest of my life longingly looking at a sport I would never get to play again.

I quickly flip the conversation her direction. "You're a Kindergarten teacher, right?"

"Oh my lucky penny! You've got a great memory! Sparkly star for you!" She lightly touches my hand, placing an imaginary sticker there.

Mental note to remove it before my meeting with more mature adults.

"Have you always wanted to be a teacher?"

"Always! Always! Always! I *love* kids. Love them. Love! Love! Love!"

A small hum escapes as I lift my cup of coffee to have a sip.

"Hate the summer time though." She slowly shakes her head in sadness. "Hate. Hate. Hate."

"Because you don't get to teach?"

Her nod is rapid though she doesn't pause for me to ask more questions. "Do you like kids?"

My mouth barely has time to open.

"Do you *want* kids?"

Yet, again, there's no time to reply.

"I have to have at least *four*." She wistfully continues although I'm not certain I'm even needed for the conversation. "And like two years apart preferably, but definitely all before I'm thirty-five. Oh! The first one *has* to come before I'm thirty."

This is far from ideal first date topics.

Bekka finally realizes I never answered. "What about you, Gideon? How many kids do you want?"

"I haven't thought about it."

"Why not?!"

"Because..." A heavy, annoyed sigh fills the space between us. "I'm not even sure I can *have* kids."

Her eyes widen in horror.

Fuck, she looks like I just stabbed a puppy.

"The trauma from the injury left lasting results in my back, leg, and fertility."

Bekka's bottom lip trembles.

Well.

This is a next level failure.

Remind me to congratulate Lenny on that prior to rubbing in her face at how horrible she clearly is at matchmaking.

Post an uncomfortable twenty-five minutes that involve me consoling what feels like a crying cartoon character, my hectic day reverts to its organized insanity. The meetings are sandwiched between checking emails and shuffling around my schedule since I'm incapable of grasping the concept that I *can't* be in two places at once. By the time I'm finally strolling through the front door of the oversized house I call home, falling face first into bed is the only thing on my mind.

"Come on!" Lenny's voice screams from the living room. "That's not the button I pushed!"

The impulse to grin grips the corners of my lips.

Coming home to Lenny is one of my favorite things. While she doesn't technically live here…she fucking *lives* here. Her tiny one-bedroom apartment downtown is an embarrassment. It lacks space. Order. And most importantly, *food*. Logically, it makes sense. She spends most of her nights here "house sitting" when I'm out of town for work, and her free time forcing me to look away from my laptop to enjoy what all my hard work has purchased. Despite the fact she has her own room here, she always ends up in mine.

56

Next to me.

Cuddling.

Snoring.

Kicking.

And giving me insomnia that can only be cured by a quick, silent jerk off session in my en suite bathroom.

It's ridiculous that she makes me feel like a creep in my own house.

Her constant, unpredictable presence is also the reason I never bring women back to my place for the night.

They don't belong here for the longevity. *She* does. Would rather her always feel welcomed than ever have her feel like she doesn't belong because of a booty call.

Strolling through my large foyer, I adjust my computer bag on my shoulder and head in the opposite direction of the vulgar shouting.

"Fuck you, motherfucker!"

Sounds of rapid gunfire combined with her rage indicate what it is she's playing.

I swing by the kitchen, grab us two ice cold beers, and trek to the main living room where she's parked on the edge of the couch mashing controller buttons.

"Take that you zombie bastards!"

The level completion screen appears just as I flop down beside her. "Lenny, why do you insist on moving the system from the entertainment room instead of just playing in there."

She takes the offered glass bottle. "I don't like it in there."

"It *belongs* in there. That's what entertainment rooms are designed for."

"It's drafty."

"Change the temperature."

"It's dusty."

"It's not. Margo and her team clean the house three times a week."

Loading music floods the speakers, and she hits me with a teasing smirk., "Then perhaps it's because I love adding anarchy to your otherwise perfectly systematic existence."

"*That* I can believe."

We laugh together and pop the tops to the bottles.

She pauses the game before propping her feet on the expensive custom-made coffee table that has the Hellcats logo carved into it. "And how was work?"

I drop the bag by my feet and take the same position. "The usual."

"But…"

My head tilts in question.

"Something got fucked up. I can tell by the way your tie is loosened."

Her observation forces me to look down at the item.

"You fidget with it when you're pissed. If it's a little too far left that means it was *your* fault but won't admit it. If it's a little too far to the right that means it wasn't your fault, but you could've *prevented* it. And if it's dead center," she motions at it, "and that far from your neck it means someone else severely fucked up, but now *you* have to fix it."

There's no use in trying not to smile.

Sometimes I forget how impressive she is.

Her attention to detail is remarkable. Always has been. It's why taking a path where she could apply said skills made direct sense. Lenny can read body lingo like it's her first language instead of third. She can coach you into confessing things you didn't even know you were hiding and build up your confidence to bulletproofing levels. While her day-to-day life typically manages to mask her phenomenal ability to connect with individuals, I know it's there.

I've experienced it in multiple capacities that started back in college with a casual comment about how being a great player didn't directly correlate to being a great person.

"Wanna talk about it?"

There's hesitation to speak.

"Sabes que quieres. You know you do."

An exasperated sigh slips out. "Junior agent fucked up a couple deals that his senior agent couldn't fix, so they want me to step up to the plate and knock it out of the park."

59

"Those are *baseball* references meaning this is an MLB situation."

"I fucking *hate* dealing with baseball players *during* baseball season."

She offers me a small grin. "Si, but it always ends with free tickets."

"True."

We clink our bottles together in a small celebratory way.

"I'll be out of town tomorrow and Thursday, so you'll have to wait to schedule your next shitty match until the weekend."

Lenny's eyebrows bounce into the air. "It wasn't shitty!"

"It was terrible."

"You're exaggerating."

"Wish I was."

"No need desear because you are."

"Unfortunately, I'm not." Stretching one arm across the back of the leather couch, I inform, "Not only was she one of the worst dates I've been on, she set the record for *shortest.*"

"How long did you stay?"

"Thirty-five minutes."

"That's not even enough time to get to know someone!"

"Wrong."

Lenny adjusts herself to completely face me. "It's not, OG. I've spent more time with taco truck vendors than that."

"Weird."

She flashes me her middle finger.

Unlike the ABC Princess I went out with earlier, she's never had a manicure.

"What was wrong with her?"

"Nauseating word choice aside?"

"¿Qué?" She pushes up her glasses. "What does that mean? She was too crass?"

"The complete opposite." I sneak a sip of my beer. "She censored herself."

"Okay, so, she's a fucking lady."

"It was like trying to engage in an adult conversation with a special guest on *Blue's Clues*."

Lenny cringes and has a gulp of her beer.

"*And* she gave me an imaginary sparkle sticker."

"Did she at least try to put it on your penis?"

"Nope. My hand."

Another wince hits her face.

"Keep the dates up at this rate, and our deal will easily be a blowout."

Her lips scrunch to the side of her mouth.

"What were you even thinking?" I continue to chastise, doing my best to include mirth in my tone. "*Please,* walk me through that fucked up thought process."

Lenny doesn't cower at the challenge, and the sight of her preparing to fire back stirs my cock.

Damn, her fierceness is sexy.

"Believe it or not, on paper you met the three out of five-bar minimum required to be connected. You actually had *four.*"

"How? Did you *lie* on my profile?"

"No," she casually replies between gulps. "You matched in core categories. You were both professionally driven, and career cemented. You both valued financial responsibility. You both preferred hard work to handouts. You both preferred making long term plans as opposed to short ones. And on a more fun note, you both love the beach."

The last line receives a sarcastic glare. "Really? The old long walks on the beach bullshit?"

"Never said walks." Lenny quickly reprimands. "Just said both of you love the beach. Which you do."

"And *you* tolerate."

"For *you.*"

My expression softens, and Mick's earlier request begins creeping through my mind.

Is this it?

Is that the boyfriend door being cracked, or am I reading too much into this shit?

And why can't women wear a flashing green light for go or flashing red light for fuck off? Wouldn't that make everything much easier for everyone?

The temptation to say something meaningful is unexpectedly squished by the shift in topic. "Wanna shoot shit in the face and blow off some steam?"

I swallow the small courage that had crept up my throat. "Fuck yeah."

"Go grab your controller. I'll load up a game."

My eyes land on the remote beside her. "That *is* my controller."

"No. That one's mine."

"No, yours is black. Mine is red."

"That's incredibly offensive." She snatches up the controller. "Just because part of my familia is afroamericano does *not* mean I have to play with that controller, OG."

Her playful tangent paired with the nickname successfully wins my surrender.

She gave it to me when some asshat who was also named Gideon came sniffing around her sophomore year. Lenny's reassurance that I was number one and would always be number one in her eyes gave me the inspiration to tell her we should try to hook up...Sadly, the day I finally convinced myself to find my nuts and do it, she was busy letting the other Gideon grope her against her dorm door.

It was a shitty start to the season that would be my last.

After grabbing my controller, a very violent, very competitive game commences. Our first round is a head to head who can kill the most zombies. Her rapid button mashing is obnoxiously impressive and her un-sportsman-like gloating gets on my last fucking nerve. The next round I vote for a rematch in headshots only mode. She over confidently agrees, assuming the same tactics will more or less work, however, having her ass handed to her unleashes the green-eyed demon that doesn't handle losing any better than I do. We curse at one another. At the screen. Drink more beer and compete for more kills. All the problems and irritation of the day are replaced with pure drive to not let my balls be handed to me in a picnic basket by a beautiful, bobble-headed beast.

Lenny loses for the fourth time in a row and attempts to throw the controller. "You motherfuc-"

"Ah. Ah." I swiftly intervene, snatching the remote out of her hand. "You're not about to break my flat screen again. Replacing this shit is expensive."

She sneers her nose.

"Wanna play something else or call it and watch Sportscenter?"

"Pretty sure they're just doing the best highlights from the season to get everyone riled up for the finals." Lenny reaches for her beer bottle. "I'd rather *play* the finals than watch reruns while waiting for them to happen."

I can't stop myself from cocking an eyebrow. "Do you have any idea how long that would take?"

"Basically, all night."

"Yeah, and I've got a plane to catch in the morning, Lenny."

"Morning like, 'hey it's eight a.m. somewhere' or-"

"Morning like my jet leaves at six."

My best friend groans her disapproval.

She doesn't see anything that early unless she's been awake since the day before.

"Fine. No Basketball. Soccer?"

"I'd rather not watch you spend two hours drooling over your Drake Lenzi avatar."

"That problem could easily be solved by you just *introducing* me to him. He *is* one of your clients."

"No."

"And why not?"

Because I fucking love her and refuse to have her swept off her feet by the biggest name in the league.

That's probably not the dating conversation segue Mick was referring to.

Childishly, I retort, "Because."

"Because what?"

"Because it would be unprofessional."

"How is introducing him to a slightly attractive admirer unprofessional?"

Slightly attractive? Try permanent blue balls level of painfully beautiful.

I brush off the question by grabbing my nearly empty bottle.

"Afraid I'm gonna go all *Swimfan* on him?"

The idea of her having sex with Drake churns my stomach. "I'd just rather you *not* join his rabbit race to repopulate the Hundred Arce Woods."

Lenny rolls her eyes and complains, "I'm starving."

"Is that why you're moody? You're hangry?"

She quickly nods.

"What do you want? It's probably too late for takeout."

"But it's never too late for tacos…"

It's my turn to roll my eyes.

"Come on! You have all the important ingredients to make me breakfast tacos."

"How do you know that?"

"It's my job to know that!"

"You bribed Margo, again, didn't you?"

A wicked smirk soars to her full lips.

Lips I'd love to have wrapped around my…

I momentarily squeeze my eyes shut.

What the fuck is wrong with me today? Why'd I let Mick get in my fucking head? Why can't I just enjoy a normal night in with my best friend without overthinking every word that comes out of her mouth? Without second guessing every glance? Without wanting to slide my hand underneath her gray tank top?

"Please, OG," Lenny's whining wins my attention. "Por favor."

Melting at the request made in a foreign language, I slowly nod, stand, and extend my hand for her to take. "Come on, loser. I'll make you a condolences meal."

She glowers at the comment but willingly accepts the declaration.

Hand in hand the two of us cross from the living room to the kitchen on the opposite side of the house.

I secretly fucking *love* and *loathe* these moments.

The ones I can pretend she's touching me because she wants me, yet loathe that she's not actually mine.

When we arrive in the room, she takes her infamous seat on the counter space while I begin grabbing items from the fridge and placing them beside the induction stove.

Just as I grab the mixing bowl from the shelf, Lenny reminds, "Remember the sal, pimiento, y ajo."

I glide over to the spice rack and retrieve the requested items of salt, pepper, and garlic. Once I've finished, I take them along with the eggs and the bowl over to where she's waiting. A mocking smirk slides onto my face. "You must really be fucking starving. That's more consistent Spanish than normal."

She shoots me a similar grin. "You know how I feel about tacos."

"*Everyone* knows how you feel about tacos."

Lenny snickers and playfully punches me in the bicep. It surprisingly rebounds into a grip. "You actually got your hair cut today."

I lightly chuckle at the comment and reposition myself between her open legs, loving the way she rarely ever sits ladylike. "And yet you noticed where my tie was hanging *first*."

"That's *obviously* more important."

"Obviously."

Her fingers slide up the nape of my neck and softly graze the edge line. "You must've gone to Shalinda." The light touch slinks around to my jawbone. "She's the only one you let shave your face." My body leans forward into the sensual caress on instinct. Lenny's index finger slides underneath my chin lifting it. "Looks good..."

Our eyes lock, and for the first time in my entire life, I do the exact opposite of what I've trained myself to. I hastily mesh my mouth against Lenny's, eyes shutting tightly preparing to endure the shame from most likely misinterpreting the moment.

When she slaps me for this shit, I'm punching Mick in the face.

The squeak of surprise is expected, but the parting of her lips isn't.

My heart hammers hard enough inside my chest to knock the wind out of me, yet I don't bother breaking away for air. Her tongue lightly searches for mine, and the unforeseen invitation to continue the kiss breaks the last of the restraint I was holding onto. I capture her tongue. Stroke it. Stroke it harder. Extract every flavor I manage to encounter. Faint hints of our favorite beer bury themselves into my senses until I'm buzzed all over again. I let my tongue sync to the spinning of my mind, losing all ability to see where the line of friendship between us ever existed. Lenny repeatedly moans into my mouth, and I desperately attempt to devour the delicious sound. One arm wraps around her figure, fingers anchoring onto her ribcage while the other roughly grips her outer thigh, both being used to tug her closer.

Keep her pressed against me.

Keep her pinned to this one scenario I've been praying for since I saw her smile at me during that fucking frat party.

Weak whimpers encourage me to slow down my movements, but the hostile hold she has on the middle of my shirt prevents me from doing so.

Our tongues continue to callously collide, crashing into each other without care or concern to what any of this shit means outside this moment, as if knowing this may be the only chance either of us get to experience this.

The possibility of that being true prompts my hand to slide higher up her thigh.

Lenny abruptly pulls back, hard nipples taunting me with brushes during her struggle to regain composure. I brace myself for the inevitable rejection. The rehearsed lines I knew would come, though I mentally begged it wouldn't be this soon. Once more, she manages to stun me. "Our deal is still in place."

Fuck…Not the best time for *that* talk.

Unsure of what I should say or what she wants me to say causes me to remain silent.

"Okay?"

No.

That's what I *want to* say.

That's what I *should* say.

Her brown eyes anxiously search mine telling me everything she's verbally not.

She's scared.

Scared of this.

Scared of us.

Scared of what happens next if we just abandon fifteen years of friendship to...fuck? Date? Do everything and anything we haven't because of the previous status of our relationship. She wants this, but knowing Lenny, going into the whole thing with a clear plan or idea or expectations will convince her it's a huge mistake.

If I wanna keep her...I'm gonna have to negotiate for it.

At least for now.

Lenny's grip starts to weaken at the same time uneasiness expands on her expression.

"Okay."

Her eyebrows lift in shock.

"*But*," I allow my touch to drift towards her inner thigh, right underneath the black baggy basketball shorts she's wearing, "only if you come for me before we leave this kitchen."

70

The hitch in her breath is intoxicating.

My fingers inch over, gently skimming the outside of her panties. A groan is grabbed over the dampness of the fabric at the same time she rocks into the touch and whispers, "Deal."

Doubt disappears allowing dominance to rightfully take its place.

I drop my mouth back onto hers, use my frame to nudge her legs wider, and glide my middle finger around the barrier. Lenny immediately attempts to lean away on a gasp, but I lash at her tongue for even considering abandonment. As much as part of me is urging that I take my time, savor the situation, live in this anomaly for as long as humanly possible, the other part…the other louder, stronger, *greedier* part is commanding I claim her the way I should've all those years ago.

The way I should every night going forward.

Wetness washes over the intruding digit, and I heedlessly thrust it forward, needing it to dive to the depths I've only dreamed of. More sharp breaths are stolen, but they barely register. My finger curls inside its new home. Commands the muscles surrounding it to clamp down. Calls to the curious orgasm in the corner to come out of the shadows and play. I push my palm against her swollen clit and use the fabric to create a tantalizing tinge of friction. Lenny's hold on my shirt goes from one hand to two. The speed at which she claws at the material slowly coincides to the one I'm executing. Her hips frantically lift to ride the increasingly frenzied motion causing the heel of my hand to heave against the sensitive nub harder and harder. My groans of hunger grow in heaviness. Force me to fuck her like it's my dick instead of my thick finger. I strengthen my hold and grind into each push with my entire body. Hers trembles at the pressure yet doesn't cease to meet the blows. Lenny's tight little pussy starts to swell around the soaking appendage, and my nuts follow suit.

Somehow, she successfully parts our mouths just enough to proclaim, "I'm coming…"

The tiny, untimed clamping I'd become infatuated with swiftly transposes to a furious pulsing that I'd previously only been able to poorly imagine. Sweltering stickiness seeps past the finger and onto the rest of my hand, searing much more than just a sweet reward into the complicated situation.

This isn't the end.

This isn't just weeks of pent up sexual frustration getting the better of me.

This isn't just the result of too many beers and not enough food.

This is every fantasy I've spent a good chunk of my life having come to a living, breathing, orgasming reality.

And now that I've crossed into the end zone, the only thing I give a fuck about is keeping Lenny like this forever.

chapter four

Lennox

The blame game.

Without a doubt the most common thing people do in harsh conflicts. I've learned the best way to handle this when it happens in my presence is to let each side get out a bit of their unresolved emotions before intervening. Most of the time, it's a very healthy part of the process, however, there have been a few occasions where it edged near violent, and I had to stop a *Maury* moment in the making.

Man, I miss that show.

Sometimes I felt he really made a difference.

"You're not *listening* to me, Heath!" Sean, his younger boyfriend, shouts.

"You're not listening *me*," Heath growls in return, hands gripping the edges of his chair harshly.

"You're not listening to *each other*," I finally intervene.

Both sets of eyes soar to me.

"Right now, you're each experiencing a different type of pain, so it is difficult for you to *understand* where the other one in coming from. Once you both *acknowledge* the other's feelings of distress, it will be easier for this relationship to move forward."

Neither of the men say a word.

"Isn't that what you want?" I pull my feet into my slightly broken office chair. "Or are you two looking for a way to end things?" The small rocking I begin fills the office with a faint squeaking. "And be brutally honest here, because that's the only way we will actually be able to make *progress*."

Heath doesn't hesitate to turn to Sean.

While I'm not supposed to have "favorite" couples, I absolutely fucking do. It's human nature! Some people you just *like* more than others, like Archer and Jaye or, in this case, Heath and Sean. They've had an interesting story. Met here at the shelter during volunteer work. Started a friendship that eventually blossomed into love. Heath, the older male, retired Marine, who never properly mourned the loss of his first husband, struggles to communicate with the younger male, Sean, a medically discharged grunt who's only dated women prior to this. Sean, on the other hand, lacks the emotional stability needed to sustain a long-term relationship. His relationship mentality of flight over fight has put strain on what they're trying to build. Their partnership is constantly developing, and both men are frequently learning.

Changing.

Growing.

It's this beautiful balance that I'm honored to be a part of.

Heath extends his open palm towards his boyfriend.

Sean offers him a bashful smile and folds their fingers together.

Afterwards, their attention falls back to me, though it's Heath who speaks. "I want us to keep moving forward. We live together, but I don't want this to just end there. I'd like us to take the next step someday. I'd like us to get married."

"What about you, Sean?" The rocking in my chair continues. "Where is it you see this going?"

"Hell, I'd marry him tomorrow if he asked." His slightly country twang causes me to grin. "But, it's hard for me to believe that's what you really want when you won't introduce me to your daughter and brush off the subject of her whenever I bring her up."

There's a heavy, frustrated sigh out of Heath prior to his confession. "She doesn't *know*."

Curiosity catches me off guard. "That you're seeing someone?"

"That I'm gay," he quietly continues, "or that her father was gay and that she's my fucking daughter at all."

Both of our jaws plummet.

"She thinks I'm just her Godfather."

"How is that possible?" I cautiously question.

"My husband...er...*deceased* husband, Gabriel, and I went to extreme lengths to protect the truth. The military was a different place when we were active. Neither of us were in positions or ranks where exposing such a lifestyle would have ended well. Once we got out, the world wasn't exactly more understanding. We did what we had to do to start the family we wanted and agreed we would tell Imani together someday, but then..." Heath swallows his sadness over the unexpected death. "Look, I know I need to tell her...I just...I haven't yet."

"Why do you think that is?"

My question doesn't receive an answer.

75

"Do you think she would reject you for being homosexual?"

"Absolutely not," Heath promptly argues. "She's very open minded. We raised her to be that way. We raised her to be accepting and tolerant of others' choices."

"Yet, I'm hearing you secretly fear that courtesy won't be extended to *you* and Sean."

Sean joins the conversation with a much softer tone. "Is that it, baby? Are you worried she's going to push you away once she finds out the truth?"

His nodding is reluctant.

I return to investigating the situation. "Because you're homosexual, or because you weren't honest with her about it?"

"The latter."

"Have you always been honest with her in the past?"

"About everything else. Yes."

"Has she always been honest with you?"

"Down to when she started shaving parts no father ever expects his daughter to start shaving."

Sean snickers at the comment. "If only she knew her father shaved down there too."

"Oh, because you don't like a smooth canvas to lick?"

The flirtation has a hand flying to my lips to catch my giggle.

This is the other reason I adore them. They argue. They yell. They cuss. But then they flirt. And kiss. And agree to try again.

It's how romantic relationships should be.

I cut a glance at the clock that's warning me their time is almost up. "Perhaps, what is happening between you is nothing more than just a disagreement on *how* to tackle the difficult subject rather than the subject itself. Here's your homework-"

"Words I swore I'd never hear again in my life," Heath grumbles.

Another small snicker escapes. "I want both of you to sit down *separately* and write your *ideal* ending to this situation. Don't discuss it. Don't even *think* about discussing it. Just write down how your happily ever after to the introduction of Heath's daughter would unfold. Next week, we'll reveal your answers, and dissect the results together."

They both nod their agreement with the task.

Here's the thing. It's obvious to *me* they both want the exact same ending. They want her to accept Heath for who he is and welcome Sean with open arms. I think hearing one another *say it* without prompting, without feeling as though the other is just saying what needs to be said to make the other happy, they will start to grasp that they're actually in the situation *together*. Often, couples need to be reminded they are indeed on the same side of a scenario before being able to make headway on the true problem at hand.

The two men sweetly thank me for my time and exit the small corner office hand in hand.

Over the past few years this little rinky-dink room has practically become a haven. On a typical week, I spend more time here than I do in my apartment. Both are covered in framed posters, although the ones here are just framed posters of classic sports icons, such as Michael Jordan, Yao Ming, Wayne Gretzky, Hank Aaron, and Deion Sanders. The posters at my apartment don't get the luxury of frames nor are they only sports affiliated. Men, which is the high number of patients I deal with, find the choice of décor comforting, while women typically assume I'm a closeted lesbian. As if all lesbians like sports and all straight women only watch them for the men they're boning. Fucking gender stereotypes and roles cause so many unnecessary headaches. The photos on the walls hide the cracks that can't afford to be repaired, the bright pink furry rug in front of my desk is a playful counter to the dingy carpet, and the lime green caboodle, given to me by Gideon in a horrible attempt to get me organized, is overflowing with a multitude of writing utensils to distract people from the notion that they're in my office to see a therapist.

Something that is still, apparently, frowned upon.

Shamed like the *Scarlett Letter* or wearing high shorts like the Fly Girls did in the '90s before it was randomly trending again.

All of a sudden, there's a small knock on my office door proceeded by Gideon's face peering around it. "Hey you."

"Hey you."

He grins widely at the greeting, and my heart lurches up the back of my throat.

Ugh.

Like I didn't have enough secret emotion problems involving my best friend *before* I let him finger fuck me in his kitchen?

Thankfully, I haven't had to see him or hear from him much since we shared that experience…*twice*, once before dinner and once after in his bed. We passed out in each other's arms that night. I was, without question, the most content I've ever been, yet the next morning I couldn't stop from wondering how fucked up our friendship would be. It's basically the only thing I've been able to think about. I've even been watching *Love & Basketball* on repeat for the past two days, rationalizing our situation to be just a new aged version of the movie. But I know that's not how life works.

No one is ever that fucking lucky.

"You ready?"

The question receives an inquisitive look. "For...?"

"Dinner."

"We had dinner plans?"

His brown eyes roll hard enough that a referee would blow a whistle for them being out of bounds. "That restaurant I told you about that I had to make reservations a *month* in advance."

Nothing comes to mind.

"The one where I told you we could order chocolate lava cake?"

"Oooo..."

"Our reservation is tonight. I've sent you three reminder texts and had Kristen send you an email."

"Phone's dead."

"Why do you even *have* a phone, Lenny?"

"Because my mother says even my abuela has one in this day and age."

Gideon lightly chuckles and shoves his hands into his pocket. "She's not wrong."

"Please don't tell her that."

This time we both laugh instilling me with a familiar feeling.

At least it's not awkward.

At least he's not saying, "we need to talk" or "hey, about the other night".

Oh shit.

What if that's why he wants to take me to dinner?! The whole let her down easy bullshit? Which I don't need, for the record! I know whatever happened was just a one off! That was clear as fucking day when he agreed to keep dating other women, something I was hoping he'd argue a bit harder against.

But why would he?

And here I am, again, needing to remind myself this is not a perfectly written romantic comedy starring my favorite actress Sanaa Lathan.

This is an imperfectly, unprecedented game involving two people who don't even play the same sport.

"Our reservations are for seven."

Right. Reservations he made a month ago…long before we ever took our relationship out of the Friend Zone. This is most likely just dinner and not a dump and dine. Though, is there anything really to dump?

Gideon makes sure he has my full intention before continuing. "It's an upscale restaurant, meaning your cut-off jean shorts and Hellcats jersey aren't going to cut it, so we should probably-"

"Cancel them."

Puzzlement immediately appears. "What?"

"Cancel them."

"Why?"

"I have my heart set on somewhere else."

"You didn't even remember where they were for! How could you possibly have your heart set on something else?!"

Leaning forward, I fold my hands firmly on my desk and tilt my head. "You're fussy. Do you need to talk about something?"

Perhaps how finger-banging your best friend is *not* emotionally affecting you the way it seems to be me?

Nope.

Not that.

Gideon glowers. "Do not treat me like a patient, right now. You're off the clock."

"And you're being catty about me wanting to cancel a dinner reservation."

"They were hard to make!"

"And *easy* to cancel."

"For. What? And I swear to God if you say for a taco truck, I will just pay for one to fucking park outside the house, so you can eat them all day tomorrow."

The slight tantrum causes me to snicker.

He starts to snap, yet realizes how ridiculous the idea sounded.

Gideon gives the neatly groomed scruff on his face a small stroke. "It's been a rough few days with work, and I haven't slept well the past two nights."

Teasingly, I state, "It's because you weren't sleeping next to me."

"Exactly."

His answer tumbles my jaw downward.

Okay, maybe he was just playing along with the joke?

"Now, I'd like to go enjoy a glass of whiskey, a great cut of steak, and watch *RoboCop* on the couch."

"Weller or Kinnaman."

"Weller, Lenny. *Always Weller.*"

I don't bother wasting effort on ceasing my smirk. "Counteroffer: Beer, wings, and foosball."

"So, *none* of what I said."

"Fine. We can watch *RoboCop* when we get home."

The corner of his lip noticeably lifts.

Wonder if that's because of *RoboCop* or calling his place home...Though it is. It always has been. Even back in his apartment days, I spent more time crashing on his and Mick's couch than I ever did my dorm bed.

"¿Por favor?" I pair the word with an overexaggerated lip pout. "Side Street Oasis is playing at The Sack, and I really, really, *really* wanna go. Do you have any idea how long it's been since I heard them play?"

"Three weeks."

Ugh. He really is like the long-lost lovechild of Father Time.

"We've actually seen them more recently than I've been to this restaurant."

"I'll pay."

He seems unimpressed by my generous offer.

"Fine. I'll pay *and* won't force you to slow dance with me to their Savage Garden covers."

"Or *any other boyband*," Gideon reiterates with a sharp point of his finger.

I cringe at the declaration. "But what about-"

"No."

"Or-"

"No-huh."

"There's-"

"Definitely not."

"Fine." My hands fly into the air as I spring to my feet. "But you should take the Lambo."

"Why's that?"

"It always puts you in a better mood."

Gideon smirks at the comment, adjusts his tie, and nods to himself.

Probably best I leave out the part about how hot he looks behind the wheel of it.

That would definitely cross us from unawkward territory back to "we should never do that again" side of the map, which is the last place I really want to be.

The next two hours fly by. Gideon changes clothes, his car, and, even less willingly, his music. I pump a wide-range of '90s classics from Usher's "Nice & Slow" to Metallica's "Nothing Else Matters" making sure to squeeze in our "Can't Touch This" duet to insure we achieve maximum ass-kicking vibes. Whenever we play sports, regardless if it's air hockey or shooting hoops on Gideon's court, we both play to win. It's why being on the same team is what's best for us...and *awful* for everyone else. Initially, we bounce around the sports bar dabbling in darts and ping pong, trash talking only one another but are eventually challenged to a double's foosball game that quickly escalates into an impromptu tournament.

"Bring it, OG!" I shout at the top of my lungs, hands frantically flying between the handles.

"Blitz! Blitz! Blitz!"

The shouted instruction is proceeded with a cross-over move where we swap handles and frenziedly spin them to trounce the other team. Our combination of yelling, slight position changing, and aggressive nature tend to distract our opponents long enough for us to score.

"Whooo!" Gideon grunts. "In the famous words of our boy Johnny Drama..."

My best friend makes momentary eye contact with me before we yell together. "Victory!"

The two men I would guess are in their later 20s grumble their grievances and toss a twenty on the table for beers.

I snatch up the bill and shimmy around with it while singing a foosball inspired parody of Britney Spears's "Oops, I Did It Again".

Gideon simply chuckles, shaking his head. "Those aren't the moves."

"Those are so the moves!"

"They're not."

"They are!"

"They're not."

"I'm sorry, were you Spears's choreographer?"

"No, I was a horny as fuck teenage boy watching a hot blonde chick move her body around in a red leather catsuit." His grin grows devilish. "Think I'd remember the way she moved around in it a bit better than you."

Snatching my nearly empty beer glass from the table we claimed not far from where we're kicking ass, I nod in agreement. "Good point."

Gideon lightly laughs again. "You want me to go grab us another round?"

I wiggle the bill again. "I can get it."

"Or I can." He snatches it from my grip with minimal effort. "Oh…too slow Lenny M who never goes soft of them…Too. Slow."

The old college rhyme he only breaks out during competitions causes me to smile wider than it should.

It's a *dumb* phrase, but it's *our* phrase.

And another sign that, despite what happened between us a few days ago, everything is back to normal.

Which is what I want.

Or…is the lie I keep telling myself *to* want.

I lean against the edge of our small square table and watch Gideon do his best to weave around the packed room.

The Sack used to just be filled with men who would come to eat wings, drink beer, watch sports, and yell obscenities at the flat screens, but about a year ago, it was bought by new owners who had higher aspirations than just a somewhat profitable man cave. Wardrobes changed. Wait staff stopped being just one gender. Weekly specials started. Themed nights that would encourage women to come hang out were pushed to the max, which included karaoke and cover bands. Surprisingly enough, the men didn't revolt. They just started cringing through the shit they couldn't stand to take advantage of their favorite watering hole doubling as a pick-up place for pussy.

My eyes stay pasted on the man I can't seem to set free, drinking in his overly-perfected frame. Even Michelangelo would be scratching his beard wondering what's left to fucking carve. His entire torso is still cut like he's expected to rush onto the field for a playoff game. Large, broad shoulders. Smooth, muscular back. Plump ass you could break a tooth on just dreaming about biting. While his lower half carries his own personal hatred, it still measures up to the top. Gideon Lucas *looks* like one he should be arranging a

86

meeting with himself for representation. Sometimes I think he pushes himself to stay that physically fit to compensate for the career change he was forced to make. Like most men, he hates to discuss anything too deep or too emotional for fear of looking weak, but every once in a blue moon I get a glimpse of the other side. The one that does pushups for the penance he feels he owes his teammates for letting them down over a decade ago. The one that buys extravagant bullshit to hide his resentment over having to deal with players who are the same age he was in the prime of his fallen football dreams. I know what fuels the ruthless agent the world loves to see because I was *there* when the seed to that monster was planted, yet sometimes, I can't help but wonder does his flame actually still burn bright with an undying love for sports or is fear of unexpectedly changing courses again what keeps him dedicated to his job.

Gideon finally manages to get the bartender's attention to order us our celebratory beers. Seconds after he's finished talking to the man, a young, undeniably attractive brunette, gently touches his elbow to grab his attention.

He immediately offers her a warm smile that churns my stomach.

Ugh.

There's his "she's cute" grin.

The female says something at the same time she tucks her hair behind her ear.

Stupid.

A stupid, predictable girl move.

It's used to draw attention to the face while projecting a false image of innocence. That whole "I don't do this often, which makes you special" bullshit. Hard to blame her, considering most men still aren't huge fans of forward women, but come on. Be more creative.

Gideon's smile remains as their conversation continues.

She gives him a flirtatious, playful push that I'm fairly certain is followed by a comment regarding his muscles.

An uncomfortable knot begins to form at the pit of my stomach encouraging me to look away.

To stop *torturing* myself.

That this is what I *want*.

I want my best friend to fall in love and have more than just premium sports packages to come home to at night.

The truth is, I want it to be *me* he falls for…

Or, if I can't have that, then to at least wait until I'm not leering at him on our date as he makes another.

Er…Not a date.

Friends don't date.

We…*hang*.

Which is all we're doing and why I'm not channeling my inner *The Craft* moment to perform some sort of spell out of jealousy.

What? No. I'm not jealous.

The brunette leans forward on a full tooth laugh, tits purposely bumping against him.

Maybe a little.

Gideon's given our beers in exchange for the twenty. He denies the need for change and turns back to the woman. His head motions my way, which prompts the female to snap hers around. Her eyes briefly narrow at me, although she keeps a smile plastered on her face. He exits her presence, beers held high to reduce the chance of them spilling. By the time he arrives back at me, the brunette has rejoined her group of friends who all look like they were just being born when some of the cover songs were being *released*.

"Wanna go to the patio?" He extends the drink my direction. "Be closer to the music?"

I try to pull my eyes off of the women who are now scowling at me.

What the fuck are they glaring at me for?! I don't even know what he said!

Gideon steps into my line of vision to make eye contact. "She was cute, Lenny, but not that cute."

My eyebrows lift.

"Besides, I'm taken."

Suddenly, my heart starts to thrum so loudly I'm afraid it's going to burst my eardrums.

"At least for six more shitty dates."

The poke at our deal receives a smirk at the same time I snatch my beer.

"And needless to say, even if I *wasn't*, she's not my type."

I steal a sip of the beverage. "Too pretty?"

"Too young." He casually has one as well. "I don't need nor want a woman in my life who can't remember life before Google." His arm drapes around my shoulder. "Also, I could never date a woman who doesn't know it was Destiny's Child who sang 'Say My Name' and not *just* Beyoncé." My laughter prompts him to add, "You may wanna write some of this shit down for reference."

We walk side by side towards the patio. "Nah. I didn't pack anything to write with."

His overdramatic gasp grabs more chuckles. "No eyeliner or glue stick you stole from a third grader?"

"You know I *hate* eyeliner. I always end up looking like a racoon or like I'm headed to the first football game of the season."

"True."

He receives a short elbow to the ribs just as we cross onto the patio where people are dancing.

Side Street Oasis has been my favorite cover band for the last three years. They consist of six dudes and a female drummer who occasionally rocks the female jams, though their lead singer's falsetto voice can definitely handle it on its own. Most of the music they play is pulled from the '90s. However, their main priority is to always make their listeners happy, which often leads to some '80s classics and popular early 2000s releases.

The opening notes to "I Want It That Way" originally performed by BSB begin to float through the air, and I hit Gideon with a familiar expression.

His head shaking is immediate.

My nodding of yes is just as instant.

Our nonverbal argument continues until I break down and grab his hand to drag him to dance. I sing along like the rest of the audience, swing my hips side to side and use my beer glass like a microphone, yet he maintains his refusal to join in by simply staring at me. Another male close to me shoots me an approving smirk and prepares to say something when I'm yanked closer to my best friend. He joins in singing the chorus, cheeks noticeably reddening with each passing word. Through my giggles, I return to crooning, though our eye contact remains.

The song transitions into Evanescence's "Bring Me To Life" and Gideon loosens up a lot more. We headbang together. Jump around. Lean into one another strumming on our beer glasses like they're guitars. He spins me around, wraps one arm around my waist, and sings the backup vocals over my shoulder while I sing my heart out to the main lyrics.

Our closeness isn't unusual, but my reaction to it is.

It's as if my senses have been cranked up to extremely heightened levels.

His aftershave is a clean smell that's subtle but brazenly demanding my nose inhales every whiff it can. The groomed scruff on his face brushing against mine sends shivers down my spine. Hell, even the way his fingers lightly touch my hip cause my breath to hitch. Our bodies swaying together feels sensual.

Sexual.

Second-nature.

It feels like we're exactly where we should *always* be.

Regardless of the song fading, Gideon remains close to me, my back pressed firmly to his front. The band plays a couple more prepared songs followed by a few requests. We're given numerous chances to pull ourselves apart during the music changes, yet we stay merged, neither of us clearly wanting to be separated.

Bobby Brown's "Every Little Step" has the crowd creating an impromptu group dance. I don't hesitate to hop out of my best friend's arms and show off my still sharp '80s choreography.

He shakes his head before removing the practically empty glass from my grip. "You can't properly do those moves with a beer in your hand. Didn't you learn that lesson the night we met?"

"That was a *different dance*."

"Same amount of fucking movement," he playfully chastises, passing them off to a dish boy. "And if you're really gonna do this song justice, you gotta get more knees into it. Like this."

Gideon joins the dance showcasing moves most people assume he's incapable of.

Gotta admit. His resolve to never let the results of his injury hinder him from enjoying life have always been admirable. No, he can't run like he used to or tackle men his own size, but there isn't much else he stops himself from doing. His limp isn't something that usually even registers to him unless someone else brings it up or his lower back pain reaches excruciatingly painful levels. Damn sure barely commands attention in my mind…I mean, at least it doesn't until he's on the cusp of outperforming me.

Laughter bounces between us as we jump around the grassy area with the other listeners. We exchange silly faces. A bit more trash talk. Concentrate much harder than necessary at times.

A shift away from the upbeat music to a slower melody has me abiding to the earlier decree. "Sounds like that's our cue."

Gideon's face flashes confusion.

"I swore no dances to Savage Garden."

He lets the corner of his lip kick upward and cuts the coupling crowd a small glance. "We can dance if you want."

"But *you* don't want."

"No man should ever *want* to dance to a song that could be featured on the soundtrack to every chick flick movie, past *and* present." Our mutual laughter is immediate, although mine stops when he takes my hand. "You know I'll dance to this shit with you, Lenny. I'd dance to anything as long as I'm dancing with you."

Oh...My...God...Who says shit like that to someone that's *just* their best friend?!

That *has to* mean something.

It's cloaked with so much underlying subtext that the inner therapist in me wants to sit down, flip through old text books, and in-depth decipher the shit like a coded *Where in the World is Carmen Sandiego* message found on the back of a cereal box.

I try to steady my voice at the same time I tug him towards the side exit. "Come on, OG. I agreed to *RoboCop*. You kept up your end. Let me keep up mine."

His reluctance to leave remains.

Our hands stay lightly linked during our stroll across the large parking lot, but I do my best not to overanalyze it.

Maybe *that's* what the holdup is between us.

Maybe I'm always overthinking rather than just letting us naturally go where it is we both seem to wanna go.

Maybe *I'm* what always truly hinders us from becoming something more.

Huh.

Don't overthink much on a daily basis outside of my relationship with Gideon.

Guess I love what we have too much to constantly be so careless with it.

The self-deliberation is abruptly ceased by Gideon's proposal. "You can drive home."

I snap my head his direction. "Were you sneaking shots when I wasn't watching?"

"No. Why?"

"Because only Too Drunk To Drive Home Gideon makes such an offer."

"That's because he cares more about arriving home alive than a little damage done to his favorite car."

"Why do you always assume I'm gonna hurt your precious vehicle?"

"I've seen your Honda, babe. It's alarming."

"Disculpa. Those are just…love marks."

"Not a thing for cars…" I toss a few daggers at him to which he responds by flashing his fancy key at me. "Swear you won't take her over ninety."

Excitement thrums through my vision. "Swear."

"Swear that you won't try to reenact that scene from *The Fast and the Furious* where Letty smokes the car next to her."

I'm unable to catch my frown.

"Real life, Lenny. I don't wanna end up spending the night pulling favors to get you bailed out of jail and charges dropped when I could spend it in bed next to you watching Officer Murphy shoot shit with really big guns." He passes the device to me. "Swear you'll be careful."

The roll of my eyes is hard. "Swear I'll be careful with your precious car."

"It's what's *in* the car that I give a fuck about, Lenny."

A response escapes me.

Once we're in his Lambo, he launches into an unnecessary explanation on how to handle it. His tone, while friendly, is firm and borderline condescending.

It's not like I've never driven a car before.

Fuck, it's not like I've never driven *this* car before.

It's only been like a year.

He continues jabbering, and I grow impatient waiting to simply *start* the damn thing.

Gideon leans over to point at a button on the steering wheel. "And don't touch that."

My head rolls in his direction. "Anything else, Bond?"

His jaw drops to rebut, yet his stare lands on my lips. The combination of closeness and attention to an area that desperately misses him ignites a starvation inside I should ignore.

Or maybe I shouldn't?

Impulsiveness gets the better of me, and my mouth feverishly conquers his. Gideon's groan is accompanied by his tongue aggressively coming after mine. I grip the wheel tighter, using it for leverage as I hastily increase the speed of my presses. Needier grumbles are given, and his hand latches onto the nape of my neck. It isn't long before the movements of our mouths and bodies become corybantic. His fingers dig into my curls, clumsily catching them. Mine abandon the hold on the wheel to paw at the crotch of his pants. We accidentally gnash teeth. Bite lips. Bump into the seat.

Embarrassment begins to seep into my system, and I swiftly attempt to banish it.

What kinda fucking woman in her thirties is *this* bad at making out?

I should've spent more time doing field studies on sex rather than reading about it. Or, at the very least, upped the number of hookups on my very low roster. In comparison to Gideon, his sex experience is very much like this Lambo. It's meant for higher class clientele. Saved only for when *he's* in the mood to take it for a spin. And makes all other drivers envious at the beauty he's pulling. Me? Definitely Honda territory. Most men are midlevel. Reliable even though not necessarily exciting. And no one's ever been jealous of the few times I *was* on someone's arm.

Fuck me, I'm way out of my league.

Come to think about it…I'm in the wrong sport all together.

My fingers flex around his hard cock on top of his jeans, and Gideon pulls away to groan, "Are you trying to get me to mess up the leather in this thing?"

A devious smirk slips onto my face. "Is that an option?"

His eyes bore into mine. "Do you want it to be?"

I let my stare shift down to where my hand is impatiently waiting to make the next move. His dick nudges against my hold as if begging me to say yes. The small, anxious action causes the response to spring free. "Si."

Gideon's growl is significantly louder than it was while we were kissing.

My attention lifts back to him, noticing the strained muscles in his neck. "You like it when I speak Spanish?"

"It's fucking sexy."

The admission has me squeezing my thighs tightly together to dull the intensifying ache. "Abrir la cremallera."

His teeth clamp onto his bottom lip.

I translate the previous command with a sexy smirk. "Unzip."

He holds my gaze hostage yet removes my hand to swiftly follow the request. Afterwards, Gideon guides his cock out of his boxer briefs revealing a sight I damn sure wasn't ready for.

My jaw drops, bobbing at the wide, thick, surprise.

How is it he just became even more flawless?

97

How is it his dick isn't slightly crooked or shorter to balance out the rest of his masculine perfection?!

How the fuck is this fair?

My best friend clears his throat in discomfort. "Um…Should I put it up? Did I misread this situation? Did I-"

I smash my lips on top of his to silence the doubts I accidentally created. He initially attempts to pull back, however, the second my palm is pressed against his shaft he abandons all efforts in that direction. His hand fists my hair once more while mine mimics the action on his cock. My mind urges me to move slow, spend more time exploring the length…the texture…the weight…but instinct spurs me to return to our previous frenetic behavior. The execution is ferociously sloppy. I stroke my tongue in sync with the speed of my fingers. Pull his bottom lip between my teeth in tandem to the gentle tugging of his balls. Salaciously suck the sting I've created at the same time my thumb rolls precum up and down his slit. Gideon savagely groans at the havoc being wreaked upon his system. The hand in my hair grips it harshly, yanking my entire body into each jerk while the other is cemented to the door handle, clutching it so hard his knuckles are turning white.

A mixture of empowerment and sexual femininity tear through my veins.

I've never felt so wanted, and so in control, before.

When we were in the kitchen, it was clear he was anxious to have me, but it pales in comparison to this moment. Then, he was calm and collected. Driven by the desire to give me pleasure. He was all the things he normally is, but now? Now he's losing, really losing, his restraint. All composure banished. Any shred of his infamous self-discipline has been dissipated. He's grunting my name like a caveman only capable of one word and kissing me like I've got the antidote for whatever sexual sickness has stolen his sanity.

I brought this out of him.

Me.

The best friend who never thought she'd be the booty.

The best friend who wants love but, in the meantime, is willing to settle for the benefits because they're the most incredible thing I've ever experienced with another person in my entire life.

A slew of fucks come spiraling off his tongue seconds prior to him crashing our mouths back together. Our tongues twist and turn, tangling into knots that have us both desperate for air.

My stroking slows to shallower brushes, and Gideon immediately growls his disapproval.

I leave his lips, which receives an even louder grumble. "Problema?"

His groan is coated in frustration and lust.

"Mendigar." I let my tongue slowly lick his top lip. "Beg. Beg me to make you come."

A ravenous rumble is released at the same time his forehead knocks against mine. "Please, Lenny." Gideon's words tremble in unison with his body. "Please, make me fucking come."

Without teasing him further my hand returns to the task like it's my new calling in life. Up and down it slides, palm slick with pre-cum, fingers flexing to provide the added pulse to feel like pussy, though my own objects to not being able to replace the appendage. His hips hastily thrust upward into the wet, hot friction, and I can't stop myself from wedging a hand between my thighs to alleviate some of the building tension. Gideon's brief glimpse of the action instantaneously becomes his undoing. He lets loose a deep, animalistic groan against my lips and shoves his tongue viciously back into my mouth. Thick cream coats my hand nearly causing my grip to slip. I moan from the steamy sensation as much as the shift in our situation.

This can't be just a two-time thing.

Those don't exist.

Once is an accident or random happenstance...

Twice is the start of a habit.

And while fooling around with my best friend is probably going to end with us *both* needing years of therapy, I'm going to enjoy every single minute we're together like this...

I just hope when it all has to come to an end, I haven't lost the one person I know I can't function without.

chapter five

Gideon

Friends with specifically negotiated benefits.

Because why the fuck wouldn't we be?

After the incident in my Lamborghini, which required me to get it *and* my jeans detailed the next morning, we spent the drive home having what has to be the most bizarre conversation we've ever had. And considering the shit we've talked about in our indiction of friendship, that's fairly impressive. Neither of us were exactly sure of how to say what it was we were both wanting to say, so it came out similar to a rookie agent trying to explain to a rookie athlete the best way to proceed with where he is in his very early career. She made a lot of odd faces and chewed on her fingernail until it was bleeding. *That,* strangely enough, is what broke the tension. My fussing about not wanting the authorities called over blood and semen being found in my car lightened everything up. We eventually came to an agreement that has been serving us both well the past few nights, even if it's not ideal *just yet*. We agreed that we could continue to fool around with one another during this dating disaster bullshit as long as none of my dates get physical. If they get physical, though they won't, everything sexually between us has to end. The intelligent and *wise* decision would've been to tell her right then and there that none of the dates stand a chance because I've been in love with *her* for almost half my life, but it didn't happen. Maybe it was due to the fact a large part of me fears this whole thing is just her scratching an itch that hasn't been scratched in a while or maybe it had something to do with us being in my bed and her hand finding its way to my balls before I could even grab the remote to turn *on RoboCop*. Whichever reason it was explains why I'm here at an exclusive rooftop lounge about to meet date number two.

The blue and purple lighting do a stupendous job in setting the sexual mood, but if you didn't come together, it makes it difficult to spot the person you're supposed to be meeting. Especially when you have no clue what she looks like because your disorganized cousin of Cupid forgot, *again,* to send you a photo to your phone so you would know what to expect.

Guess I could take part of the blame since I have the password to check the email account that would provide such information, but it's easier to pass the blame to the woman so busy trying to juggle helping Vets, helping her family, and "helping" me that she forgets to charge her phone.

My eyes scan the leather booths currently being occupied by just one person. Some are quickly joined by men carrying drinks while others have females flock back to them indicating girls' night out.

Lenny has never been a big fan of those.

Boys night out?

Absolutely.

She loves beer, wings, and long talks about why trading Dereck Devety to the Wellbourne Warriors was the dumbest move the San Del Sol Sharks ever made.

But girls' night out where they squeeze into something short, order fruity cocktails, and gossip about their sex lives? She'd rather jam a mascara brush in her eye. Thankfully, the female friends she does have aren't exactly big on that shit either. When they hang out, they typically just eat pizza and watch the chick flicks I refuse to.

Despite Lenny's childish taunting, it doesn't make me a Neanderthal to refuse to watch *Crazy Rich Asians.*

102

I don't care for romance movies unless they have a direct sports tie-in, like *Love & Basketball* or *Jerry Maguire*.

I mean…only a soulless monster wouldn't love *Jerry Maguire*.

He fucking had her at hello.

My attention finally lands on a woman who's in a booth all alone towards the back of the lounge. Adjusting my suit jacket, I slowly make my way towards her hoping this isn't her, so I can say the woman was a no show and go home to Lenny sooner than expected.

Upon my arrival at her table, she grows a devilish grin. "Gideon Lucas."

"Ciara Chu."

The attractive Asian woman gives her slender, sleeveless shoulders a small shimmy. "Don't I look like my profile pic?"

How the fuck would I know?

Instead of ruining the date instantly, I shoot her a grin back. "You look better."

She winks at the compliment at the same time I sit down in the booth seat across from her.

"Don't you wanna sit next to me?" Ciara offers, hand patting the empty space beside her. "Don't bite…unless you want me to."

I force my smile to remain. "Prefer to know a woman for longer than thirty seconds before I let her sink her teeth into me."

Ciara giggles at the retort and pulls her long black hair to one side of her face.

Alright. In the looks department, Lenny did good...*again.* She's clearly in excellent shape. Arms toned. Tits small but perky as they pour out of the burgundy cocktail dress. Skin silky smooth from a glance, just like her hair. Her stare is dark yet projects confidence, something that is quite sexy to most men, me included.

"How about I get us a drink?" I offer politely.

"How about you let me serve you?" The retort rubs me uncomfortably, although she doesn't seem to notice. She stands and instructs, "Make sure you watch me walk away. I'm dying to know if you approve."

There's no need to ask what she's implying.

Pretty sure I'm hearing what she's screaming loud and fucking clear.

Ciara strolls away towards the bar with my eyes pinned to her perky backside.

Not bad.

Not bad at all.

Not nearly as incredible as the soft, round one I woke up to pressed against my dick this morning, but under prior circumstances, it's definitely one I wouldn't have minded sitting on my face.

Fuck, what I would give to have Lenny sit on my face.

It doesn't take more than a couple minutes for her to grab us drinks, and when she returns, she decides to sit in the space next to me rather than her seat. Ciara pushes the glass towards me, tiny chest doing everything to be noticed during the process. "Hope this is okay, sir."

The emphasis on the word "sir" plays to my early conclusions.

I slide the whiskey into my grasp while asking, "What are you drinking?"

"Whiskey sour." My nodding receives follow up information. "I like the way it *burns...*"

Oh...It's without a doubt going to be a long date.

Instead of taking the bait to walk the path it is clear she wants me to, I extend one arm around the back of the booth and ask, "You work in marketing, correct?"

She quickly nods. "Marketing executive for Wilcox Whiskey."

"Is that what we're drinking?"

"Is there anything else *to* drink?"

We exchange a small flirtatious snicker.

"It's a great company." I compliment. "How long have you been with them?"

"About seven years but got the promotion I deserved only a few months ago." Her head and smile both become crooked. "Nowadays, I spend my days playing with the big boys and making sure to be on my knees for them at night." My eyebrows launch into the air causing her to quickly correct. "*Not* the men I work with...but...*other* men in powerful positions." Ciara's touch drags itself along my forearm. "*Sir.*"

I push down the growing discomfort. "You're looking to be someone's submissive."

"I'm *made* to be someone's submissive."

Gotta give the woman this. She's in charge of her sexuality, and that's admirable.

When I don't immediately flirt back, her tone loses the lightness, "Look, Gideon, I am an extremely busy woman, which is the primary reason I'm using this fucking app to begin with. I work ridiculously long hours *most* days of the week with a very unpredictable schedule. I make so many decisions in a day you'd think I was trying to run a fucking small country rather than just a division of a corporation. During the little downtime I do have, the last thing I want is to have to *think*. I just wanna be able to *feel*. Follow. Have someone else be responsible and focus solely on providing me with pleasure. So..." She gives my arm another stroke. "Are you interested in being my *daddy*, or am I wasting my time?"

Her bluntness, though surprising, is something I can appreciate.

Turns out I might get my wish on going home early after all.

My response isn't what she was hoping for, but also isn't one she flat out accepts. She insists we finish our drinks since they're already paid for and simply enjoy each other's company. We touch on easy topics like sports, which she has absolutely no interest in. Movies, though the only films she'll watch are foreign. And food, from which I learn she's a vegetarian. Her sexual antics continue throughout the conversations, ending only once I've walked her to the valet station and declined the one-night stand proposal. The valet boy who overhears the comment seems unable to stop shooting me looks like I'm insane for passing on such a precious piece of pussy.

If only he knew what was already waiting for me in my bed.

I arrive home even more exhausted than I was when the date started thanks to a pit stop at one of Lenny's favorite taco places and an annoying construction detour that added fifteen minutes to the trip. During the walk to my bedroom a dull pain begins to spread in my lower back. The obnoxious on again-off again aches have gotten worse as the years have gone on. I've done a fairly great job hiding it, because trusting your career to a man who appears weak due to a limp is hard enough, but trusting your career to a man who has trouble walking altogether is idiotic. How can a man who can't take care of himself ever take care of *you*?

"Maldita puta pasar el la pelota! Pass the ball!" Lenny shouts at the top of her lungs.

The sound instantly brings a smile to my face.

At least I know there's one person who has never thought my injury makes me less of a man.

Pushing the door open to my bedroom, my eyes immediately drift over to where she's sprawled out in the middle of the mattress, on her stomach, face supported by the palm of her hand, and eyes glued to the flat screen that's pinned on the wall.

A familiar announcer's voice causes me to chuckle my question, "Are you yelling at *highlights*?"

She snaps her face in my direction. "They're forcing me to relive the shitty game, so I'm allowed to relive my earlier reactions."

I flash the fast food bag in my clutches. "You can yell from the bed, but you gotta eat on the floor."

"I'll be careful!"

"Lenny, you're never careful, and the feeling of shredded lettuce in my ass crack is not one I've forgiven just yet."

Her snicker is attached to a short shrug.

Glad she thinks it's cute.

It's not.

Your bed is not your dining room table. It's not meant for *food*. And if you do bring food to it, it's supposed to be in the form of a whipped cream bikini, thank you *Varsity Blues*. *That* is not only sexy but can be licked off, as well as easily washed off, your sheets.

No one finds rolling around in lettuce sexy.

No. One.

"Speaking of my bed," I toss a nod in its direction, "what the fuck did you do to it?"

Her attempt at pretending to be innocent is awful.

"Why are my sheets one color and the pillowcases another?"

"They're Hellcats colors!"

"I don't need to sleep in them. I'm not their mascot."

She bobs her head in a mocking fashion. "How about a thank you for buying me new sheets?"

"How about I didn't *want* nor *need* new sheets?"

"Beg to differ after what happened between us this morning…"

Yeah, I imagine getting cum out of my sheets was probably not something she wanted to ask Margo to do…

Why is it instead of just washing them herself, Lenny opted for the wilder option of buying something new?

My best friend crawls off the mattress, snatches the bag from my grip, and sets up shop beside the foot stool at the edge of the bed. "How was your date?"

"You're getting *worse*."

She lets out a theatrical gasp. "She was *perfect* for you."

"Yeah, if I had a sex dungeon I needed to put to good use."

"You do. It's in the basement. It's just been so long since you used it, you've forgotten it exists."

My head tilts at her, only slightly amused.

"What was *so wrong* with this one?"

"You know I'm all for women who enjoy taking charge of their sexuality-"

"You sweet feminist."

I helplessly roll my eyes. "*However,* when I feel I could probably write up a sexual harassment suit against you, it's a problem."

Instead of chomping into her soft chicken taco, she cringes.

"What led this match to happening, and *please,* don't say it was career based again."

"Okay then. I won't say it."

She bites into what I'm assuming is dinner rather than just a snack.

Her eating habits haven't progressed much since we were in college. She still has a tendency to spend more time munching during the day then remembering to eat ridiculously late or only when reminded by me that she needs a real meal. It used to happen because of her studying schedule, classes, and work. Now, it's because of helping her mom repaint the house, working at the clinic, and playing part-time cupid.

I know it's dumb to think, but sometimes I like to believe she *enjoys* me taking care of her. Making sure she gets dinner. Buying her new sneakers when it's clear hers have given up. Holding her close when she has a nightmare.

They seem like little things I shouldn't think twice about.

Yet occasionally I do.

Walking over to my dresser, I begin to undress, starting with my watch. "Go ahead. Explain this match to me."

"Ciara was career driven. Focused. Had corporate aspirations I thought you would admire. I mean she's one of the only female marketing executives at this huge company *and* the youngest they've ever hired for such a position. She was committed to putting in the work to climb the ladder, ya know? It reminded me of how dedicated you are to pushing A+ Athletes from being number four in the country to *actually* being number three."

"We *are* number three."

"You're number four."

"Number *three*. We demanded a recount."

Lenny shakes her head so hard her curls bump into her face.

After I've emptied my pockets, I rest my back against the furniture. "Do you think work is the *only* thing I'm interested in?"

She ceases her attempt to eat once more to tilt her head sarcastically at me. "OG, you're basically bullying me into a job I have no desire to take because *you're* overly concerned with career stability, so I think it's a safe assumption to conclude that you would want a partner that possesses that same business-related aspirations in *their* field."

She's not...*wrong*.

Damn it. I hate that she's not wrong.

Lenny continues to lecture with a mouth full of food, "It's a totally natural human instinct for someone to want their mate to match their level of ambition." She swallows and smacks away whatever taste is lingering. "Back to Ciara. She was too aggressive?"

"Too aggressive...and then there was the fact we had *nothing* in common."

"*Nothing?*"

"She hated sports, meat, and movies that were spoken in English."

"Yikes."

"Yeah, pretty fucking awkward. May have surpassed crying Rapunzel for worst first date ever."

"No," Lenny quickly denies, wiping her hands. "Neither of those win for worst first date ever. *I* have the worst first date ever story to end all worst first date ever stories in this friendship."

Relationship.

I want her to fucking say *relationship*...

I stroll over to the stool to sit closer to her and insist, "Hit me with your best shot, Rocky."

"You mean *Creed*. He was black."

"The jab wasn't racially motivated. It was about knowing your cocky ass is coming into this conversation and going to lose."

She lightly laughs, pushes her dinner aside, and faces me. "Get ready to endure a knockout, baby."

My lips press together to stifle the groan that grows any time she uses the term.

"Couple years ago, Archer set me up with one of his co-workers. It was similar to the set up you went through tonight. I was all about beers, tacos, and sports while he was all about wine, sushi, and home improvement projects."

"You hate sushi."

"Be a fucking man and put el pescado in a fucking tortilla."

I don't bother hiding my laugh.

"*Anyway*, he took me out to Swinging Sushi. Aside from the fact of having nothing to talk about and there being *nothing* on the menu I wanted to eat, he ends up disappearing for a *really* long time to the bathroom. Like food poison level of dump time. I go to check on him but then hear moaning from the women's restroom and get distracted. Do a little investigating, because uh, hello, who doesn't love a little voyeurism, only to discover him in the stall, fucking a waitress, who I later found out was his *ex-girlfriend*. He only brought me there to make her jealous. It worked. Oddly enough, after our date they got back together and ended up married last year."

112

Bewilderment overtakes my expression. "How the hell have I never heard this story?"

Lenny gives me a small shrug.

"Why didn't you tell me when it happened?"

"You mean why didn't I let you go to the store, pretend to need his assistance, and then kick his ass in the back?"

I don't refute the prediction.

"There was more important shit to deal with at the time."

"Like what?"

"You had just come back into town after spending a week trying to close the deal with some whiney rookie who decided not to sign, which was the worst mistake of his career, and needed to vent. And drink. And have your very bruised ego stroked."

The corner of my lip threatens to tug upward. "Was *your* ego not bruised?"

"Yeah, but I rebound better than you on and off the court." Lenny laughs harder than I do at her joke. "You needed me more than I needed to bitch about some dude they had to twist my arm to go out with."

Initially, the comment causes me to smile, yet the action quickly fades back into a frown.

Has it always been this way? Has she always put her own needs on the backburner to put mine first? How many times has she needed me to listen that I haven't? How many times in all these years have I stopped to really hear her like no one else makes time to? Am I ever really giving her what she deserves in a deep conversation or just waiting my turn to talk?

A sharper ache pierces my lower spine forcing me to grit my teeth.

"You okay?" She swiftly questions.

"Leg's a little stiff...Back's been hurting like a bitch today."

Concern in her eyes expands exponentially. "What'd the doc say at your last appointment?"

"Pop two pills a day and call me when you need a refill." The grunt that leaves me is bitter. "Same shit he's been saying for years."

Despite knowing how much I hate pain killers.

"Want me to help massage it?"

Her offer is a welcomed surprise. "You don't mind?"

"Have I ever?"

"Because I want you to rub me, I won't pull at that thread."

She gives my non-sore leg a gentle nudge, stands, and saunters away to the en suite bathroom to retrieve the cream. I silently shed my clothing until I'm down to just my boxer briefs. By the time she returns, I'm leaning back on my palms, pushing harsh breaths out of my body to bulldoze through the pain.

Lenny lowers herself between my thighs and lifts the container of medication cream up towards me. I swipe a small scoop to rub on my back while she begins to spread it on my leg. We work as a team to alleviate as much pain as we can. The actions bring back fond memories the way they always do. She's first to begin the reminiscing of my physical therapy days, and I'm quick to add to the humorous experiences we engaged in.

114

The entire time wasn't bad. While I had been abandoned by everyone who realized I was no longer a meal ticket to them, me, Mick, and Lenny became family. They doodled profanity and provocative images on my casts. Helped me scratch the itches inside with odd objects. Scared away women who only wanted to throw me sympathy ass once my dick was in working order again and led those with more class my direction. Lenny went to therapy with me whenever she could. Mick drove me around like a fucking Uber. They proved they had never been there for the future fame, and it was during that experience I knew they'd be around for the rest of my life.

Lenny's fingers dig in deeper to the tissue, and I try to catch the groan before it can leave my lips. She shoots me a wicked smirk. "You want me to do it again?"

My stirring cock begins to fully swell.

"Maybe a little...*higher*?" Her hand slides to my inner thigh and massages firmly. "Am I high enough yet?"

I hate having to retort, "As far as you can go with that cream on your hands."

Her tongue snakes out to caress her lips, and I lean forward wanting to chase after it.

"How about I use something else to massage your cock? Like my mouth?"

And here is the *perfect* example of how I want my woman's sexual aggression to be shown.

Using my clean hand, I free my dick from the cloth prison. The cool air is only allowed a single caress before it's disappearing between her full lips. Lenny plants her grip firmly on my thighs and begins a barbaric bobbing. She lacks the erotic grace given by someone who does this regularly. However, her frantic movements

115

are packed in a fierceness I find sexier than perfected skill. Heat from her hollowed cheeks sears my shaft, yet it's the spit dripping down to my balls that has me possessively growling. My fingers bury themselves into the curtain of curls and clamp onto a handful. Lenny squeaking around the tip of my cock prompts me to pull her to me. The tip of my dick tickles the wet haven in the back of her throat and stopping myself from pursuing more of the forbidden territory is inconceivable. I viciously thrust into her throat, receiving a gagging sound I could spend an eternity jerking off to.

"Relax those muscles, babe," I immediately coach, not wanting to abandon the wet, hot paradise I'm in the process of claiming.

Lenny grumbles her response.

The vibrations only add to the pleasure, which spurs me want to dive deeper. "Don't fight. Let my dick slide down your throat like it's home base."

My analogy has the positive result I was anticipating.

Her fingernails cut into my flesh for traction, yet her throat unconstricts to receive more of me. The invitation to fuck her face seems too good to be true. Too good to be real. Too good to fall into what must be some sort of dream trap. As if able to sense my apprehension, my best friend picks up the pace of her sucking once more.

I groan at the way my shaft is suffocating in the soaking confines and return my stare to a stupefying sight. Lenny maintains a steady speed, the tip of her nose in a competition with itself to reach the base of my cock. Each time she shifts the slightest sliver closer, my balls curl up in anticipation of rewarding her with a well-earned prize. Choking sounds reverberate around the room in stereo. They evolve in intensity, and my growls match in savagery. Lenny's cheeks work wildly to maintain the delectable suction while I cruelly push her to the breaking point. She unexpectedly peers up at me, brown eyes watery, mouth spread wide from my cock, and spit smeared around like game day face paint. A long, slow moan is offered up like a Hail Mary pass. The combination of the beautiful vision and even more beautiful sound shatters me.

Powerful burst after burst rush down the back of her throat prompting me to say, "Swallow for me, baby. Swallow every. Last. Fucking. Drop."

Lenny gormandizes my cum, moaning louder each time she succeeds in following the command.

My entire body trembles and shakes through the lapping that proceeds my orgasm. Her tongue swirls around my shaft, searching for lost remains and sucking up lingering flavor that may have been left behind.

I struggle to keep the grip on her hair.

I struggle to get air back into my lungs.

I struggle to ignore the increasing ache in my back.

Being with Lenny this way wins over any level of agony that my body has the balls to throw at me. I don't give a fuck if it means I don't walk right for the next two days or have to actually use the pain pills or even start physical therapy again. This woman is worth giving everything I have and everything I am to. That's a fact that'll never change whether we end up being more than this shit or not.

chapter six

Lennox

"Do you plan to actually eat any of that mustard or just wear it?" Gideon grouses.

I finish smacking on the bite of the ballpark hotdog currently in my mouth before overdramatically licking the lost yellow condiment off my thumb.

"That's disgusting."

A small laugh slips loose at the same time I dip my index finger in the paste. Immediately afterwards, I turn to my best friend and attempt to smear it along his top lip. "How about you wear it too?"

He doesn't hesitate to block and dodge.

See, here's the problem with having a boyfriend who is not only well acquainted with sports, but really good at playing them. He can bob and weave like fucking Ali.

Oh shit...

Did I say boyfriend?

I didn't mean *boyfriend*.

I meant, guy friend who I'm almost boning and wish was in love with me...When are they gonna come up with a term for that shit? Bonefriend? Wovefriend? Bowovefriend?

"Stop it, Lenny," Gideon grumpily grumbles. "You're gonna make me spill my beer."

"Then just sit there and let it happen."

He swats away my hand, the look on his face teetering between disapproval and amusement. "Do you have any idea how offensive that sounds?"

"Shut up." I lightly chuckle without abandoning my efforts to paint his face. "You know you love this."

"*Again.*" Gideon catches my wrist. "Very Law & Order SVU of you to say."

My leg bumps into his causing the beer to slosh around his plastic cup.

"Hey!" He releases his hold to rearrange his beverage, and I use the opportunity to sneak strike his lip. Unfortunately, I barely get more than a small line near his nose. "Damn it, Lenny!"

Another snicker slips into the hot summer air surrounding us. "It's like a baby Hitler mustache."

His glower deepens.

"I was going to go for more of Mr. Monopoly thing, but fuck it." I return to munching on my hotdog. "I'll take what I can get."

Gideon mumbles his irritation, snatches a spare napkin from my lap, and begins to clean the area. "That shit can dye your facial hair if it sits too long."

"You don't want blonde highlights?"

He narrows his vision.

"Guess you wouldn't look like your profile pic then..."
Seeing an opportunity to make a segue, I finish up the last of my
favorite baseball food and take it. "And now that you brought it up-"

"*You* brought it up."

"How was your breakfast date this morning with Hannah, the
successful entrepreneur, whose hobbies included a love of knitting?"
My eyes dart back to the field where the other team's up to bat. "She
manage to crotchet her name on your heart?"

Please, God let the answer be no.

I mean *yes*.

No...I mean no.

As much as I don't want to work at some soul sucking job
that will inevitably feel like another prison, I don't want him to fall
for someone else more. I honestly don't even want to keep tempting
him with women who possess actual potential to be a good match. I
keep rehearsing speeches where *I* tell him we should just forget
about this shit and give us a shot, but they always come out jumbled
and end with the imaginary version of him telling me good joke or
good game, not taking my word rambles seriously. Therefore, I want
him to tell me this deal is stupid, and that we're stupid for continuing
to do it, and then kiss me like his life depends on it...Which is the
only way he kisses me. Every time it's happened, it feels as if he's
trying to pour his soul, his entire reason for existence into me. It's
overbearing. Overwhelming. But, most importantly, overzealous.
He's never *phoning* it in.

Those are the worst kisses.

I'd know.

I've endured and delivered equal amounts of them.

After watching the player completely miss the ball, Gideon answers, "You should just give up now."

My head snaps in his direction in curiosity.

Is this real?

Is he about to give me some heartfelt speech secretly written by Karen McCullah and Kirsten Smith, the women who wrote the classic *10 Things I Hate About You*, that more or less wraps up the whole movie?

Is there about to be a music cue followed promptly by a kiss and credits rolling?

"You really are *awful* at matchmaking."

So...nope.

Not time to release the doves or breathe easier.

Defensively, I bite back, "I'm not *awful*. No soy."

"If it were baseball, this would've been your third strike, and this whole thing would be over."

Yes, and if we were normal adults instead of two stubborn ones, we'd sit down and wade through the difficult discussion of what's happening between us rather than just writing it off as two best buds borrowing a little friction in the sheets.

"The date was a disaster."

Score!

"Is that like the only word in your vocab?"

"It was an atrocity."

"Oh…Way to knock that one out of the park. Unlike the Bayridge Bears." My head motions to the game. "I thought they were having a great season."

"The Highflyers are having a better one."

I smirk at the retort and reach for my own beer that I placed near my feet while eating.

Despite the old saying regarding baseball being the best American sport, it's one I *tolerate* more than enjoy. Up until a few years ago when Gideon became an agent, I always just changed the channel. My father is a die-hard basketball fan along with both of my brothers. Never really understood the appeal of this game or the need for the long-ass innings. Even Gideon had to grow to love it, which progressed without real resistance. Sports and all things sports-related come natural to him. Memorizing regulations, legends, current players, and stats is all second nature. I like to think sports are his first language and English just the one he learned to convey his love affair with them. Baseball is still something I find incredibly boring, but live games are much more enjoyable than watching it at home. Plus, I live for ballpark hotdogs, cotton candy, and ice-cold beer on a hot summer day. The team jerseys we're gifted every year to wear like super fans are just a fun, flashy bonus. Although, from the way Gideon keeps glaring at mine, I take it he's not particularly thrilled with the way I've bunched it to one side giving it a sexier look. As much as I *wish* it were to tempt him into taking me to the parking lot and finger-banging me in the front seat of his Escalade, it's only something I do to keep cool. Kinda like sporting the baseball cap on my head. Then again, if *that* was really to keep my face from overheating, I'd wear it frontwards instead of with a *Fresh Prince of Bel Air* twist.

Gideon loudly proclaims, "Hannah was a crazy cat lady."

The comment causes me to meet his stare again.

"Not exaggerating."

"She's an animal lover."

"No, she's an animal *hoarder*. Twelve cats is too many."

"¿Doce?" My voice squeaks. "Did she think they'd be cheaper by the dozen?!"

Gideon chuckles and has a sip of his beer.

"Are you fucking with me?"

"No." He wedges the cup back between his legs. "I saw pictures of all *doce*. Just listening to her name them had me feeling like she was gonna skin me in the diner bathroom to make a human rug for her preciouses."

Cringing is the only response I can muster up.

"Oh! And she was ten minutes late because her *pet sitter* was running behind, and she couldn't leave her babies unattended."

"They're los gatos…Don't they watch themselves?"

He shrugs. "You would think."

"Okay, so aside from her love of cats-"

"*Hoarding.*"

"-why else wasn't it a match?"

"Putting aside the disgusting amount of animal hair she was covered in that also fell into her food to which I then watched her *eat*," he describes with an appalled expression. "There was no…chemistry."

My fingernail momentarily lands between my teeth.

"She was...*painfully* shy. I had to ask the majority of the questions, so we could do more than just *stare* at each other while waiting for our food. She had a shit ton of passion regarding her pet grooming business but not much else. She was only into movies that featured animated animals because of the horrible things pet actors endure, and modern music was something she avoided since her cats only preferred the soundtrack *to* the musical *Cats*. When I asked her about her hobbies, she did mention knitting, yet said it's really just a game she likes to play with them by *pretending* to knit while they bat around the ball." He doesn't let me comment. "Was she an option because she *too* had a great zest for business?"

"Actually no," I hum between beer sips. "I listened to your concern about business being your only mutual interest and went a different direction. You both shared a love of animals."

"I don't have a...*love*...of animals per say."

"OG, the only charities you donate to outside of those that provide assistance to the youth are those that help endangered animales."

A small blush burns his cheeks.

Yeah...the big, burly sports mogul has a soft spot for creatures who can no longer protect themselves.

"Plus, your favorite movie growing up was the first *Free Willy*."

"He was just a kid who saved an animal from being murdered! He was a goddamn superhero in the making."

I give his thigh a comforting pat.

Gideon rolls his eyes yet lets a small laugh leave his perfect lips. "Fine. I can...*understand* your logic."

"Gracias."

"But she was a miss," he firmly states, stare boring into mine. "And I have no doubt the next four will be too."

Wonder if me being on the list like Carly suggests will change his tune or if I'll suffer the same fate as the others...

Redirecting my attention back to the game isn't difficult knowing I'd prefer to focus on a lighter, easier to navigate topic. We watch together in comfortable silence. The crowd around us buzzes with chatter, some game-related, others food-centered. A few parents fuss at their children who have become uninterested in the sport and dancing mascot while others make promises of cotton candy or foam fingers if they'll just make it to the seventh-inning stretch.

Casually, I ask, "Did I tell you Winnie is pregnant again?"

The mention of my little sister's name causes him to roll his head in my direction. "Does she know she's not a goddamn gumball machine?"

"I don't think she got that memo."

"Maybe you should write it *to her* in *ink* instead of lip stain?"

His playful suggestion receives a chuckle from both of us. "Mom's thrilled. Dad's already swearing they won't keep watching the kids like free childcare, though, they're not the only ones feeling that sting. There are moments when I think I spend more time parenting those kids than Winnie and Diego."

"That's gotta be true. Putting aside how you pick them up *from* school, doing school projects, and making sure they either have lunch money or their ideal lunches made, you also practically guide them through the ways to survive being emotionally unstable because they're three, four, six, and seven."

"All kids are emotionally unstable at their ages. There's a chemical imbalance that plays a factor as your brain is developing."

"You know so much weird shit."

"Aw," I playfully coo. "Gracias."

Gideon chuckles prior to inquiring, "How do your brothers feel about it?"

"Mateo is thankful his daughter isn't the youngest any more, and Gordon is requesting they all stop having children because he doesn't make enough to keep up with buying all the Christmas presents he already has to."

Gideon's smirk is surprisingly fleeting. "Do you...ever think about...following in Winnie's footsteps?"

"Do I ever think about having enough children to start my own rock band? No."

He slouches down a bit in his seat. "I meant about *starting* a family."

I lift my eyebrows in bafflement, ill-prepared for a question I never saw coming.

"You know, you're worried about *me* settling down someday, but what about you? Do you..." his hand drifts upward to tug at his collar, "want...any of that? A house? Kids...?"

Gideon's nervousness is almost as startling as the question itself. If he were sitting in my office, and I took a moment to observe his behavior from body language to tone, I could conclude there's an

126

underlying fear to it all. A worry, though it's hard to decipher over what exactly. Does he wonder what will happen to *us*, to our friendship, if one of us does end up hitched to someone else? Does he secretly feel that's going to be me, and he'll no longer have a place in my life? Or maybe…maybe he's afraid those are things he wants to be the one to provide for me, but can't?

"Stop gaping at me," he grunts, redness blooming across his tanned skin. "I simply asked you a question, not to solve a complex riddle."

His snide comment encourages me to kick the side of his foot with mine.

"Hey! These are limited editions. Don't Lenny them up."

"Did you just *verb* my name?!?"

He cockily tilts his head. "I did."

Swiftly, I repeat the action with a little more force.

"What the fuck did I just say?! You know, Elio hates having to scrub these."

"Then maybe you should stop paying your wardrobe assistant to clean your shoes?" The suggestion spirals me to snip more. "And maybe you shouldn't *have* a wardrobe assistant? Maybe you should let your everyday shoes and clothes be *less* pristine. Maybe it wouldn't kill you. Hell, maybe it would help to alleviate all the pressure you constantly keep yourself under to be 'perfect'."

His mouth bobs, yet he doesn't successfully speak.

"No one's perfect, Gideon. No matter how many little details you nitpick or how many times you get something cleaned or no matter how many times you *overthink* the preparation process, there will be blemishes. Things will get a little tarnished. Damaged. Worn.

127

That's *life*. And that's okay. It's totally acceptable to relax and get your hands dirty more often than you do. Especially if you want to be a father someday. Kids are…insanely messy. They literally shit on schedules and vomit on plans. They have no care or concern for the clock that isn't the one *they* internally follow. You're gonna have to learn to keep the anal-retentive, overthinking shit in the office because once you step through your front door, your son or daughter or both need you to be flexible as well as able to make prompt decisions." I lift the last of my beer towards my lips. "And yes, I want that chaos someday…"

Gideon's voice is barely above a whisper. "You know I can't have kids, Lennox."

"That doesn't mean you can't have a family."

My retort is met with a wrinkled forehead.

"Fostering. Adoption. Those are both great ways to grow one. Just because they don't carry your DNA doesn't mean they're not yours."

Hope appears in his warm, chocolate glare. "Do you think you could settle for those?"

"Absolutely. Though, I would never consider those options as 'settling' so much as just taking a different path."

The lack of vacillation shifts smiles onto both of our faces.

"Foam fingers!" Yells a vendor. "Get your big foam fingers!"

I frantically wave my hand in the air. "Over here! Over here!"

He darts toward me, weaving around whining children whose parents are glaring at me for bringing the temptation closer. "What can I get ya?"

"Two foam fingers, please."

"Two?" Gideon grumbles. "One for each hand? You gotta know how stupid that's gonna look."

"One for each of *us*," I correct and grab cash out of my back jean-shorts pocket. "I'll take a silver one."

"And for you sir?"

My best friend shakes his head.

"He'll take a black one. Matches his mood."

"Fuck you," he huffs under his breath.

The vendor chuckles and exchanges the goods for the money I'm holding out. He begins to count out the bills he should give back when I insist he keeps them. The man thanks me for the tip and moves on to other fans who are now wanting to purchase the accessory.

"Put it on."

Gideon repeats his previous denial.

"Put. It. On."

"No, you bite-sized bully. You're not gonna push me into meeting your demand."

"You're right." I slide the bulky object onto my hand and shove it at his face. "I'm going to *poke* you into it."

He laughs at the lame joke against his own volition before swatting it away from his face.

My poking continues, although I alternate attacks. Not having much space to wiggle around in allows for me to successfully strike his nose, his neck, and his ear. Gideon repeatedly curses at the actions and demands for me to cease the playful onslaught. Eventually, he caves and grabs his foam finger to even the fight. Back and forth we duel. Odd jabs taken. Strange slashes warranting theatrical scoffs. Our laughs grow increasingly louder along with the attention on us. I use unfair tactics like smooshing his face with my free hand to deliver rapid pops to the chest. He takes each one like a champion, allowing me to appear triumphant in a fight that could've easily been won by him with minimal effort.

All of a sudden, our antics are halted by the sight of an inside the park homerun in action.

We can't shoot to our feet fast enough. At the top of my lungs, I scream, "Correr! Correr, you magnificent bastard!"

"Run!" Gideon shouts the word in English from beside me.

Arturo Rodriguez sprints towards home while the defensive team scrambles to stop the play. The moment he crosses home plate, our entire section screams in elation. The announcer gushes about the beautiful play at the same time Gideon and I embrace each other in excitement. We squeeze one another too tightly. I wiggle in thrill. He pats me in happiness. Our bodies begin to part, however, he ceases the separation by dropping his mouth onto mine. My free hand grips the edge of his shirt, always needing something to support my weight under the intense pleasure that turns my knees into Jell-O. His teeth nip at my bottom lip requesting entrance, and the moment I oblige, his tongue invades to reiterate not only the joy of our team winning, but the bliss over being able to kiss me as part of the celebration.

The only thing I may have to "settle for" is our friendship.

It's stolen moments like this I'm not sure I can go back to living without.

130

chapter seven

Gideon

Over the years, my love of suits has grown similar to the way my love of less popular sports has. Once upon a time, I didn't give a shit about surfing or MMA fighting, but, like most things in life, that *changed*. My career was, of course, the reason for both, learning quite quickly that extreme athletes are just as profitable to represent though often much more fun to be around, and that in order to be taken seriously as a professional you have to *dress* like one. A little dispute that has never been put to death between me and Lenny. She insists, "Clothes do not maketh the man." Arguing, "It is the man that maketh the clothes.". Then proceeds to lecture that if we would decide collectively as a society that sandals and board shorts were how a Congressman should dress, not only would it be the new attire, but it would have no effect on their ability to do their job. Or avoid their job...depending on the day. These little tangents are always attached to my request she wears the *one* cocktail dress she owns. The dress I bought her *specifically* to slip into for these types of events. I've even replaced the damn thing four times in the past year alone because of the stains she "accidentally" keeps getting on them. Her stubbornness is fucking irritating.

And, in an unusual way, adorable.

"Are you gonna finally tell me what was wrong with Andi with an I?" Lenny questions from the other side of the closed bathroom door in our hotel suite.

The fidgeting with my cuffs continues. "After the event."

"Originally, you said *after* a good night's sleep."

To which I insured we both got with a little sixty-nine action that kept me covered in the smell of her until we showered this morning. *Together.*

Fuck, every day should begin and end with my face between her legs.

"And then you said *after* we got on the plane."

I wasn't lying. The intention was to put her through the ringer over the latest horrible dating adventure, but work required my attention. She shouldn't complain. My apologies came in the form of letting her stream *Clueless* and stuff her face with doughnuts.

"When that didn't happen, you said *after* your meeting with Mick."

He wasn't at all surprised I ended up bringing Lenny, however, that wasn't the sole focus of the conversation. One of our potential clients who is doing the Taking Too Long to Sign Tango had the balls to demand we take a smaller cut at the same time insisting he knew a *better* agent who would. While Mick is still a pretty good agent, dealing with direct bullshit is not his forte any more. He's very groomed in the actual business side of everything. What to do with the money that's coming in. How to increase our reach. Our value. Our brand. He has versed himself in the aspects of *controlling* a company, and I focus on the agents. I'm the one who deals with their struggles. The one who spares them the "I understand" bullshit to tell them to pick their nuts up off the floor and get back to work. Most of the time, I lead by example as well as set the bar for what they should be trying to reach. Occasionally, I coach them to get better results or step in to insure a deal that would benefit us all if it goes through. Mick and I are two halves of a powerful machine. He knows how to handle his breakdowns. I know how to handle mine. And putting a buck-toothed, backwoods, barely able to order the beer he enjoys guzzling baseball player in his place was a walk in the park for me. The awkward conversation regarding

133

the status of my and Lenny's relationship, on the other hand, could've sent me into a whiskey-induced coma.

"But then, when you got back here, you insisted I start getting ready or we would be late to this thing."

"Which we will be if you are just now starting your makeup like I *know* you are."

There's a short pause proceeded by a small huff. "I wanna hear about fecha número cuatro, or I'm not leaving this bathroom."

My head falls back at the building exasperation. "We do *not* have time to play this game, Lenny."

"Better get to fucking talking then."

I shake my head in silence.

Would it kill her to just do the shit *I ask* every once in a while?

Is it not enough I'm still going out on these ridiculous escapades just to guarantee she takes this job I know she really wants but is, *again,* too stubborn to admit it? Is it not enough that we're going her speed with all this shit, though I'm not complaining about it? Taking Lenny little by little feels like opening the spaces on a Christmas countdown calendar. Each little discovery builds palpable anticipation to unveil the greatest gift of them all. Assuming she doesn't just decide that we're knocking at the door of Too Complicated and should back away before we fracture the foundation of our friendship.

Pretty sure it's already begun to crack.

"You think I'm bluffing," she says slowly. "You really wanna take that gamble with what's on the line tonight?"

134

I toss the door a harsh glare.

Fuck, why does she have to know me so well?

My body moves towards the closed door at the same time I begin to explain, "Andi, with an I, was…atrocious."

"Too vague."

"She met me outside the restaurant, though refused to let valet park her car because she doesn't need a man to do that for her. The reservations were under her name since, as a woman, it's important that the world knows your name is just as important as a man's." I brace my back against the door frame and return to fiddling with my lucky cufflinks. "I can respect those views, however, the ones she gave for her decision to not shave her arms or her pussy, to not wear deodorant or lotion, and to just brush her teeth with water were a bit too much for me."

"Oh…no…"

"Oh…yeah…" Disgust creeps into my expression. "Look, I can respect a woman who wants to burn her bra and refuse to trim her bush, though I personally don't want my dick exfoliated, but someone who doesn't use toothpaste or deodorant because she doesn't like the way it affects her body chemistry and preaches it's just one more way the men of corporate America are trying to control the female population…isn't the type of woman I want to be the mother of my children." My head turns towards the door. "Maybe that makes me the world's biggest dickhead to want a *cleanly* woman to raise my children. Fuck it. I'll willingly take home the award if that's the case."

"Poor hygiene choices…" Lenny says, snickers snuck in between her words. "Is that…all?"

"The unibrow was a bit off-putting, although it was the constant spew of hatred for men, an overly gender biased society, and refusing to be another cog in the oppression machine that really made me skip dessert. There's only so many times a man wants to be verbally kicked in the balls as he becomes a scapegoat for his *entire gender*." My hands slide into my pockets. "Oddly enough, I understand how Andi with an I was picked. She was a strong woman, with strong values, and principles she not only believed in but was willing to fight for. I do admire a woman with that level of strength." Lenny's face begins to flutter through my mind. "A woman not afraid to go against societal norms, not afraid to swim against the current, not afraid to be…who she truly is despite the possible repercussions." A lopsided grin begins to grow over the idea this woman was the closest to Lenny so far. "She was an epic fail, but it wasn't hard to see how this match was made."

All of a sudden, the bathroom door swings wide open revealing an unbelievable sight.

The words rush out of my mouth in a jumble, "Holy, fuck…"

Lenny strikes a comical model pose while my eyes scramble to drink in the heavenly creation. Her sleeveless floor length dress is black and white. Its flowy nature is almost easy to forget with the way it clings to her chest as well as the open cut-outs on the sides that wrap around to provide an almost backless gown. From her ears dangle turquoise accessories that look like they should clash yet somehow manage to add a pop of color I didn't know was missing. There's a matching ring displayed on the hand she's using to hold her silver clutch. Her curly hair, that's unfamiliar with blow dryers let alone other heating tools, has been primarily straightened. The thicker curls on the ends have clearly been added in after the fact and having it all dangling to one side of her flawlessly made-up face has my fingers itching to run through it.

"While you were busy having dinner with the second coming of Frida Kahlo, I was busy letting Jaye and Carly *She's All That* me." She uses her index finger to push her glasses up. "Minus the losing the glasses bit. I need mine. My face looks like a deformed Hershey's Kiss without them."

I want to argue it doesn't but can't seem to convince my mouth to move.

"I know you were just expecting to treat us to manis and pedis, which, by the way, thank you again for, Jaye hasn't been that nice or that peaceful in *months*." Lenny scrunches her nose. "Even Archer says he owes you one for the surprise outing. Pretty sure my future nephew may be a demon because he's definitely making me wonder if his mother is gonna actually give birth or need an exorcism instead."

Although I still don't speak, I do manage to laugh.

"I um…Well, I thought since this dinner thing was a huge deal, you'd want me in something nicer than the one LBD you repeatedly replace like a dad who keeps stepping on my hamster when I'm at school."

That's a grizzly analogy.

"And…I…wanted you to be *proud* that I'm your date. And I wanted you to…be…*impressed*." The nervousness floating in her tone is endearing. "Kept the receipts in case you hated everything, I could return it. *Except* for the makeup. Apparently once you open that shit, it's yours." She instinctively lifts her nail to chew on it but swiftly stops when she catches a glimpse of the manicure. Lenny forces her hands to her side and questions, "What do you think?"

I finally manage to unravel my knotted tongue. "I think I'm the luckiest man alive to have you in my life."

An unusual redness creeps into her cheeks.

For a brief moment, we simply stare into one another's eyes.

Now would be the ideal time to say all the shit I need to say. To thank her for going out of her way to try to please me because she grasped the magnitude of this situation. I want to praise her for following through with the request to glam herself and remembering to swing by the office to grab my credit card to do it on my dime, but then chastise her for leaving me a note to grab more beer written in highlighter. I want to tell her loyalty to me never goes unnoticed, and that allowing me to pamper her makes me feel like a fucking man. A man who not only handles his shit in the boardroom but at home too. This would be the perfect opportunity to say how much I love her and want for her to be on my arm at every event as my *wife* rather than my best friend I'm *almost* fucking. I should say all that and so much more. Right. This. Minute.

"You look beautiful, Lennox."

She shyly smiles. "And if you check your very expensive watch, you will see that I am ready *on time* for once."

"Proving you are capable of reading clocks."

My snark receives a small swat to the shoulder with her clutch.

I bend my arm for her to take and the two of us head out of the room for the elevator. When we reach it at the end of the hall, she gives my bicep a soft stroke. "You know you look good too, right?"

A small chuckle escapes. "Thanks. This bowtie makes me feel like I should be waddling along the coasts of Antarctica."

"Can I call you Happy Feet?"

"No."

"But-"

"Lenny."

The playful scolding causes her to concede. "Fine. But only because I know you need to stay focused on impressing Barrett Gallagher so that he will give you his consent to sign his sixteen-year-old son. Barrett Gallagher Jr., who has broken state high school records. Be fair warned, Barrett Jr, who prefers to be called BJ, apparently has his mind focused more on getting his stick touched than touching an NHL stick."

I lift my eyebrows in question just as the doors ding open for us to step inside. "How do you know all that?"

"His Instagram account reads like a remake of an *American Pie* movie."

"You did research?"

"Of course, I did." Our descent begins. "On him and his emotionally-distant, yet pays to pretend they're super close, padre."

"And you know *that* little tidbit, how?"

"Quick Facebook look. All the photos are posed. He's missing from almost every one of BJ's games but has paid for the entire team to enjoy yacht weekends and private chef parties. He has a tendency to treat his son like a trophy he enjoys polishing and showing off. He lacks actual emotional investment, which probably eats him up somewhere deep down inside. This means if I can portray a partnership with you as being the parental figure he cannot seem to be, he's more likely to sign."

Astonishment anchors itself into my expression.

"You play the facts and figures game. I play the people." She tightens her hold. "It's why we're a dream team."

Can't argue with that…

Downstairs in the ballroom where the charity event is being held, we waste no time making our way around the function. I smile for cameras and mingle among a few familiar faces. Lenny is silently glued to my side, yet the constant closeness fills me with unusual confidence. While I don't *need* her to be a pretty doll that other men are envious of, I appreciate the trust in letting me lead rather than fighting for the reins. These aren't the type of people she deals with on the daily. They're the ones she hears me gripe about. Occasionally encounters and then mentally gives them a textbook label. They're often the type of individuals she flees from as well as the type she worked with before abruptly quitting. Most of the events I drag her along to she's still allowed to be some version of herself. There are always athletes to poke fun at, most of which adore her fun spirit. There's usually finger foods to distract her from the politics at play or catchy music to help her tune out the diplomatic insults exchanged. This is the epitome of everything she hates in one room…but she didn't hesitate to come nor has she complained about being here. And her strong, silent support she's offering with forced smiles is a sign of true devotion to our friendship.

To our unusual new relationship.

To me.

It isn't until we arrive at the silent auction tables that I get my first glance of Barrett in person. It's not a shocker that he looks exactly like the headshots I've seen. In fact, he actually possesses more of a dickhead arrogance up close. The way he carries his slender, fit frame doesn't show signs of an actual sports-related past, and I have to refrain from expressing my displeasure.

Parents who were never athletes are so much fucking harder to deal with. They typically come in two categories. One who wants their child to be everything they weren't so they push too hard, too fast, and wreck what could be a valuable player, or they brush it all off, blinded to the skill and dedication required to *be* a true athlete.

140

"Uh…creep alert," Lenny mumbles near my ear. "Gallagher has his hand on his wife's hip but attention on that waitress's ass."

My eyes follow his line of vision.

"I know I shouldn't find that shit shocking, particularly 'cause she does have a nice culo but have a little fucking class," she gripes. "At least don't let your dick get hard next to your wife *while* staring at someone else."

I shoot her a disapproving glare. "How the fuck do you know his dick is hard?"

"The dropped hand technique."

Unable to resist investigating the claim, I cut him another quick glance only to discover the hand not holding his wife is blocking his crotch.

"It's not the subtlest method for blocking wood."

"But effective."

"But is it really if the woman knows *why* you're doing it?"

Her point bobs my head side to side. Suddenly, intrigue hits me, and I question, "Why do *you* know that move?"

"Oh, you and Mick have pulled that shit since we basically first met. I think the first time I caught on was when some dance chicks decided to host an impromptu yoga session in the middle of the courtyard. You could practically hear every dude in a fifty-foot radius get hard before dropping his hands down."

I'm unsure whether to cringe or chuckle.

"There you are," Mick's voice shifts the gears of the conversation. "Surprised I'm just now running into you." He gives

Lenny a puzzled look. "Aren't you going to introduce me to your date?"

"You know if *She's All That* was written in this day and age, she probably would've punched Dean in the face for being a dick about seeing her in a swimsuit or at the very least kneed him in the balls."

"Lennox?" His forehead wrinkles at the same time he leans closer to inspect. "Seriously?"

"The one and only."

"Which is probably what's best for the world. Pretty sure it would implode if there were two of you," Mick teases. He snatches a champagne glass from a passing server and tilts it toward her. "You look…amazing."

Despite the compliment intending to only offer her kindness, jealousy latches onto the nape of my neck forcing me to lower my grip to her hip. "She does."

Mick cockily smirks at the action. "Sure you've told her that already, right?" His glass starts to inch towards his lips. "After all you tell her *everything*…"

"Always has," Lenny proudly states. "Always will."

Almost everything.

The whole been in love with you basically half my life thing is the only exception.

I redirect the conversation to safer ground. "Where's Minnie?"

"Mingling with the other Mrs. Talking about…shoes or nails or hair or something chicky."

"That's incredibly insulting," my date gripes.

"It's incredibly *true*," Mick retorts. "Once they realized who my wife was, it was the only thing they cared to discuss." He has a small sip of his drink. "It's like being married to a Dallas Cowboy Cheerleader in the '90s."

"Man, those bitches were the shit," Lenny crassly adds.

"That's what I'm sayin'," Mick promptly agrees. "It's like as soon as the world knows who you are, that's the only shit they wanna hear about."

We nod our understanding.

"Have you spoken to Gallagher yet?"

I shake my head, stealing another glimpse. "Soon."

"Damn right soon. We're sharing a table with him."

"Of course we are…"

Mick's arrogant grin returns. "Don't worry. You'll have plenty of time during dinner to charm him into signing a contract. We should probably start to head that direction."

"What *is* for dinner?" Lenny curiously interjects.

"Think they're doing sushi."

Her scowl sends shutters through us both.

"You handle that," Mick points to our unhappy friend, "and I'm gonna wander over to our table."

I toss him a glare before she slips out of my grasp to block my vision.

"Let me get this straight. I've had to smile in condescending asshole's faces, pretend I give a fuck about vacations in the Hamptons, and endure incredulous looks as they try to figure out what race I am, only hanging onto the hope of an incredible three course meal only to be given *fish*?! El pescado?!" Her mixing of language causes my hand to cascade down to mask my stirring cock that is incapable of resisting the way the words roll off her tongue. She shoots the action a wicked smirk. "Really? In the middle of an ass-chewing, cabrón?"

My shoulder shrug gets a chortle from us both.

Can't help it.

Her fiery nature blended with her Spanish spewing never fails to get my dick's attention.

"Sweeten the pot, OG," she swiftly demands. "Give me *something* to make all this a little more worth it."

"What do you want?"

"Complete access to the room service menu."

"Done."

"One premium channel movie."

"Nothing in the *romance* genre."

"And for you to treat me like you would any other date at the end of the night."

The last request furrows my brow. "Meaning?"

144

"Putting my heels in the air and giving me a reason to call you *papi*."

My jaw fumbles to the ground in pure disbelief.

Did she…

Did she…

Am I fucking dreaming again?

Is this another stress dream where the first part is all fantasy then morphs into something so horrific only a PB&J can calm my nerves?

Lenny steps forward and drags her finger down the front of my chest. "Deal o no trato?

Ill-prepared to provide any counter offer, not that I want to, I press my lips near her ear and state, "You'll be *screaming* papi until your throat is raw." The sound of her breath suddenly becoming unsteady slides a smug smirk onto my face as I slip back into her direct view and offer my palm. "Shall we?"

Her hand drops into mine, eyes still wide in anticipation.

Even if this agent deal falls through, this will still be the most magnificent night of my life.

At our table, Mick takes it upon himself to begin the introductions. Barrett isn't bothered by his forwardness nor does he seem impressed. Waiters promptly deliver lettuce wedges along with champagne refills while my business partner drones on about saving the bees, which is apparently what the event is supporting. It's clear Barret is uninterested in the cause, yet his wife hangs onto every word out of Mick's mouth like it's gospel. Minnie's thankfully more preoccupied with my date's vegetable poking than she is with being jealous that another woman is fawning over her husband.

"Something wrong?" Minnie questions Lenny from across the round table.

Lenny sends her stare to Mick's wife. "Just waiting."

"For?" She swiftly inquires.

"The waiter to bring out the tortillas and meat to go with these toppings he's placed in front of me."

Minnie hides her snicker behind her hand.

I toss Lenny a chastising glare. "You *know* they're not serving tacos."

"Then why else would they put this shit in front of me?"

"It's a salad."

"This is what my taco meat eats."

"Well, at least you know tacos don't grow on trees."

Barret unexpectedly laughs at the exchange. "You two…" He wags his finger in our direction. "You two, I like."

Mick does his best to hide his disappointment.

"You remind me of the men I like to golf with."

"Fifty bucks says I can swing better than they can," Lenny playfully retorts.

I place down my fork at the same time I join the teasing, "He's probably talking PGA not put-put."

"Screw you. My put-put score is *always* better than yours!"

146

"You cheat."

Her jaw hits the table, yet Barret chuckles even louder at our antics. "How long have you two been together?"

"So long they're practically married," Mick unnecessarily points out.

Lenny doesn't let him get away with the snide comment. "Except he's already married to *you*."

"Well then this is awkward," Minnie joins in on the joke.

Although Mick chortles, he still shoots Lenny a glare.

"Years of friendship aside, that's basically what it is when you run a business together," Lenny begins a segue I wasn't expecting. "That's what marriage essentially is. A contract between two people, agreeing to love and honor and value one another for however long you can uphold the agreement. Business...a *strong* business that's co-owned often must operate the same way, which they do. At A+ Athletes, Mick's role is definitely wining and dining and making sure the bills are paid on time-"

"Did you just make me a housewife in this analogy?!?"

The table chortles, and Lenny continues, "And Gideon, is hands on. He does more than negotiate amazing deals. He provides guidance to the players as well as all other agents he encounters. He's like a father in the sense he's concerned with more than just the zeroes you're adding or stopping him from having on his paycheck. He wants to see you grow. He wants to see you push yourself. He wants you to surpass his high expectations. He's not only passionate about what he does but endlessly dedicated to making sure each person he encounters gets a *win*...whatever a win means to them."

My best friend's speech stuns the table silent.

That's not at all what I was predicting she'd say.

A good word here. An ego stroke there. But that…That was heartfelt. Almost eye-opening to see how she sees me. I know she hates being pushed, which led me to assuming part of her loathes me for doing it, but after hearing the last line, I get the feeling it's quite the opposite.

She *needs* me to push her.

She *relies* on it.

The same way I need her to loosen the death grip I have on the steering wheel of life.

We are a dream team, even when we're not thinking about it.

Barret's wife, Melinda, is first to speak, "I love that…I love that *tremendously*."

Her husband promptly agrees. "I think guidance is excruciatingly important with younger, impressionable players, especially the underaged ones like my son."

"You have a son?" Lenny fakes her surprise perfectly. "How old?"

Barret ignores the round of waiters who are swapping finished salads for individual plates of sushi rolls and answers warmly, "He's sixteen. Plays varsity hockey at St. Virgil."

"Hockey, huh?" My date continues to prod, exciting Mick by the growing gleam in his eye. "Any good?"

"He knows his way around the ice," Barrett cockily announces.

"Well enough to go pro?" I ask making sure to keep my tone even rather than eager.

He slightly shrugs. "Maybe."

"Maybe?!" His wife shrieks. "He was the *only* freshman on the varsity team last year. He's broken I don't know how many records in his high school's division *and* club hockey, which he plays year 'round to stay sharp!"

She begins listing more of her son's achievements to which I deliver the majority of my attention. Out of the corner of my eye, I take notice of Lenny stabbing the rolls with her chopstick, to which I respond by nudging my foot against hers under the table in a silent demand for her to stop. She does; however, the ceasing of one childlike action leads to another. Lenny clumsily fiddles with her utensils turning them into drumsticks at one point, and I assist her in properly repositioning them, all the while addressing the piqued interest in an agent Barrett has begun to show. Once Lenny seems set, the conversation dives deeper. Mick takes out his phone and prepares to put an appointment for a visit with his son on the calendar. I do everything possible to keep my focus on the conversation, but Minnie's giggling goads me into investigating what has her in stitches.

The moment my eyes land on the sight I can't stop myself from joining her.

"Welcome to the party, pal," Lenny states to the sushi tower she's created on her plate.

"God, I forgot how awful your Bruce Willis impression is," I lightly laugh.

"That was golden!" She points a stick at me. "Beats the shit out of yours."

149

Accepting the challenge immediately, I quote the same line, although it's Barret who laughs at me first.

"That was horrible, too," he joins in. "You gotta have more of an edge to it."

Barret gives it his best shot, and his wife swiftly shakes her head. "Awful."

"Super awful," Lenny backs.

Mick rolls his eyes in annoyance, yet sits back to let us be entertained by the change of topic.

On one hand, I can understand his frustration. He wants to talk shop. Lenny wants to play. He wants to seal the deal, and she appears to be hindering the process. But that's the thing about Lenny. She *knows* people. Reads situations. Truthfully, she's helping in ways that my partner is too blinded to see. Her gaiety relaxes the room. Makes the conversations feel less tense and stale. Each time she intervenes with a humorous distraction, Barrett warms up and welcomes the progression of the alternate subject. She's providing a good balance to the business-only nature Mick is displaying.

She's gonna help get us the win.

And tonight, as soon as we get back to our room, I'm gonna give her everything I promised.

Dinner proceeds with more plates of sushi, more glasses of champagne, and enough laughter to make the surrounding tables jealous. By the end of the meal, Melinda is sloppy drunk, and Barrett is ready to take full advantage. We wait until they've dismissed themselves before the four of us exit the event to head up to our rooms.

In the elevator, Mick loops his arm around his wife's waist and compliments, "You ladies did remarkable tonight. Minnie, you had Melinda practically begging you to join her for a ski weekend and Lennox, you somehow managed to bro your way into Barrett's good graces."

My eyes narrow in his direction, but I don't bother putting him in his place since it's obvious I'm more offended by the backhanded remark than she is. However, if she shows *any* sign of outrage, I will quickly remind him to watch his mouth.

"Wasn't the *ideal* approach," Mick continues, "but it worked."

"It *was* the ideal approach," Lenny snips. "You seem to be the only one at the table not picking up on the no shop-talk policy he was throwing out there."

He tilts his head in question.

"Mick, Barrett is a business man. He's pitched business shit all day, every day, meaning if you actually want to get his attention about it outside a boardroom, you're gonna have to come in under the radar."

All attention diverts to her.

"I wasn't joking around because I'm incapable of being a professional snob-"

"You kinda are," I interject.

"Incapable of being a snob? Aw, thank you very much, OG."

My chuckle is accompanied with draping an arm around her bare shoulder.

"I kept the conversation light and fun to cleverly drag him the direction you needed him."

Another smirk clips onto my face. "You read the situation."

"Before we ever stepped foot in it." She displays an all-knowing grin. "There's a lot that can be learned about a person through a little bit of research into who they are and not just the companies they run."

Mick hums thoughtfully and nods at the notion.

"When do we collect our commission checks?" Minnie playfully questions.

"You can collect yours from me right now." Mick wiggles his eyebrows as the doors ding open to their floor. He gives his wife's ass a grab and tosses me a devilish grin. "You can give Lennox hers."

Her finger soars to her teeth seconds prior to the elevator shutting.

For the next minute it takes to reach our floor, neither of us speaks.

Lenny gnaws nervously on the nail she no longer needs to keep in perfect condition while I take a moment to evaluate the remainder of her body language. Aside from her anxious tick, she seems sexually tense. Her breathing is labored. Eyes hooded. Thighs clenching. Clutch-holding hand choking the object. All of these are things I've begun to notice happen whenever she's thinking about us in *less* of a friends-only manner. They're also clear signs that the thoughts are soaking her panties.

We're granted access to our floor and stroll out side by side.

Inside the deluxe, luxury suite, she slowly saunters away from me and over to the living room area. "God, I hope this fancy shmancy place has tacos."

152

I keep my pace to a lingering speed, admiring the delightful view of her toned ass subtly showing its true shape underneath the loose material. "How do you *not* know already? Isn't that what you had for lunch?"

Lenny tosses me a look over her shoulder. "I didn't *have* almuerzo."

My eyebrows pinch together in confusion.

"You have any idea how long it takes to put this shit together?" She waves a finger down her body. "Think Olympic level of commitment." A small smirk crosses her expression. "And now I'm going to eat like the champion I look like."

She begins to lean over the edge of the couch to reach for the menu that's resting on the coffee table but is abruptly pulled against me instead. Her gasp is caught by my hand clenching around her throat. I roughly angle her face to capture her lips with mine. The harsh bite of her bottom lip grants my tongue access to reaffirm dominion over an area I've had to wait all evening to enjoy. Lenny's mouth fights back, determined to maintain some level of control, yet completely concedes when her head is jerked backwards by the hold on her hair my other hand has managed to grasp.

Our sudden separation is proceeded by me guiding her body to the position I plan to take her in. "Bend over and brace your legs on the arm of the couch. Spread 'em wide."

"Si, papi."

The taunting response threatens to have me coming before I can even get my slacks off.

Lenny gathers her dress, crawls onto the edge of the couch, and rests her palms on the cushion. Afterwards, she glances over her shoulder, anxious for her next instruction.

153

My eyes remain pinned on hers, and I take my time to undo my belt. Despite the developed pain of having my dick receive a zipper imprint from being pressed against it too long, I drag out the process, wanting her to be as close to the fucking edge as I currently am. Her attention swings back and forth between observing the hunger that's increasing in my glare and watching me finally release my cock. The instant my pants and boxer briefs fall to the floor her entire body eagerly rocks backwards in a silent plea to be fucked.

I gradually bunch together the material blocking my path and let a predatorial grin pierce my expression. Once the fabric has been completely collected, I'm able to see a sight that would've had me ending the night much sooner had I been aware of its existence.

Our eyes connect, and Lenny impishly states, "Didn't want any lines."

My stare falls to the carnal situation cultivating.

No panties.

No hair.

No rubber.

Just bare.

Just one hundred percent, pure unfiltered fucking.

Her hips shift, and the hotel lighting illuminates the slickness waiting to be claimed by my cock.

And *only* my cock.

My fingers burrow into her round cheeks, and I use my thumbs to spread the doors to paradise wide open. "I'm gonna have you like I've never had any other women, baby."

154

The announcement receives a whimper.

Instinct to just dart inside battles with the need for me to take the extra minute to watch our lives change. To document to memory the moment we became what it is we've always been destined to become.

Mates, in every aspect of the word.

I guide the tip of my dick to her soaking entrance and briefly tease the area. "Beg."

Lenny whimpers once more at the same time she attempts to force me inside.

Pulling back nearly kills me. "Beg for it."

She throws a hard glare over her shoulder in protest.

Her stubbornness even in the midst of sexual eagerness makes me smile widely. "Let me know how much you want it."

An all too familiar gleam grows in her eyes. "Por favor, papi. Tómame. Romperme. Hazme gritar tu nombre."

The animalistic growl that escapes pales in comparison to the savage thrust I supply. White, hot heat envelops my cock, and my balls clench tightly, preparing to come already. I clamp down on the inside of my cheek to prevent the pending embarrassment. The new ache serves its purpose to distract from the pleasure pulsating around my shaft. Lenny moans for more in Spanish and against my own volition my dick nudges deeper to deliver it.

Being with her is unlike anything else I've experienced. With other women there wasn't a difficulty to control my actions. There wasn't a burning urgency to come inside them. There wasn't this gritty, unbridled need to have them crying out that their pussy, their heart, their fucking *soul* belonged to me.

Driven by barbaric notions my body is determined to execute, I drive into her harder, sounds of wet flesh slapping against wet flesh singing salacious praises in our erotic sanctuary. The dip in her arched back is defined. Her breath is growing choppier with every heavier heave. She whimpers for mercy in English yet cries for the opposite in Spanish. Lenny struggles to remain on her shaky limbs throughout each blow, and the beautiful display of her unable to withstand the sexual assault has me on the verge of coming all over again. I do my best to ignore the bemoaning in my balls to relish the way her ass is crashing into them. My eyes feast on the view of my dick repeatedly stretching and molding her pussy to be *me*-shaped. Quivering and quaking under the pressure of *my name* being carved onto her sacred walls.

Lenny finally confesses what it is my cock has been desperate to hear. "Estoy tan cerca, papi. So…fucking…close…"

I sharpen and shorten my thrusts. Let them transpose from somewhat rugged to completely vicious. Our bodies continuously slam together in savagery, both on the brink of being bruised from the force. She cracks first. Calls out my name in rapid succession like it's an invocation. Like I'm the saint that will provide her indemnification if what's happening between us doesn't end in the ideal scenario we have our minds wrapped around. Her pussy thrums in an incorrigible thirst it wants my cock to quench. Following suit, I come, Lenny's groans in tandem to each brutal blast that fills her.

When she unexpectedly collapses forward, she exposes my softening dick to the cool air, yet presents a view so bawdy it immediately starts to stir again. Seeing my cum smeared across her lower lips has me declaring, "Let's get that pretty pussy to the bedroom. There are heels I promised to put in the air."

Lenny wiggles her face across the cushion until she can meet my stare. Instead of requesting a moment of reprieve or whining for her favorite food, she simply lets the corners of her lips curl upward as she states, "Si, papi."

Whether or not she's ready to acknowledge it, we just sealed the deal of a lifetime.

A deal I am more than willing to do whatever necessary to make sure it never ends.

chapter eight

Lennox

I put down the neon green crayon we used to color the princess's face. "And what color should we make the sky?"

"Pink!" shouts Rainne.

"Going for an early morning vibe at the castle," I announce as I reach for the color. "I dig it. Very Mufasa in the clouds."

"Mufusa," Rainne repeats, her hand rapidly moving back and forth across the paper.

"Has she seen the original kid friendly version of *Hamlet* better known as *The Lion King*?"

"Too little. Worried some of those scenes with Scar would give her nightmares, and it's already a battle to keep her in her own bed."

Jaye attempts to color the clouds white only to have her daughter push her hand away. "No tankto."

She lets her shoulders plummet. "Really? Mommy can't color with you and Aunt Len Len?"

"No."

Her swift answer receives a shake of Jaye's head. "Unbelievable. My first-born hates me already."

I shoot her a sympathetic smile. "She doesn't hate you. We're just *bonding* here. She's teaching me that she understands Princesses can come in all types of colors, and I am teaching her not to let her creativity be stifled by the expectations of society by encouraging her to color wherever *she* feels compelled to color on *her* project."

"Why do I feel like we're having a therapy session for my toddler?"

We engage in a small snicker together that's cut short by the sound of the front door opening.

"Daddy!" Rainne squawks at the same time she takes off from the coffee table where we're coloring.

"Rainne!" Archer calls out in return, swooping her up into his naturally tan arms. He leans his forehead against hers and smiles wide. "I love you."

Her tiny nose nuzzles his. "Lub ubetoo!"

Jaye doesn't bother to hide her jealousy. "Ugh. Won't let me color with her, but you get *all the love* she has? What kinda ugly stepmother BS is that? Why is she treating me like I made her scrub the floors and sweep the chimney instead of letting her create art and eat cookies?"

He adjusts his daughter in his grasp on his way into the living room. "Rough day?"

"Every day is rough when you have a daughter who wants nothing to do with you and an eighty-pound baby playing trampoline on your bladder."

I know offspring can't get that big in humans, but now I'm curious, what's the biggest baby that's ever been born?

Archer offers her a small grin. "Is it a little easier with a husband who'd hang the moon by hand for you every night if you'd let him?"

"No."

The cold response receives a chuckle. "How about Rainne and I go play in her room for a bit and let you and Lennox have a little space?" He tosses me a warm head nod. "Hey, Lennox."

"Hey."

"Sorry to do this to you and Gideon but looks like we'll have to cancel BBQ and boardgames on Sunday."

"What?" Jaye unhappily growls.

"They're gonna need to me to come in to catch up some things that have fallen behind...I was going to explain it to you later-"

"But thought me overhearing as you tell it to my best friend would be better?"

Archer cringes at his mistake. "That's not – I should've – I meant to-"

His ramble is interrupted by his toddler daughter. "Pay wit me, Daddy!" She places both hands on his cheeks. "Pease..."

"Let me make sure Mommy doesn't need anything first."

Rainne frowns and plops her head on his shoulder.

"Do you?" Archer questions his wife. "Other than a little breathing room from the tiny one and to hear more in-depth on why I

160

had to cancel, do you need anything? Water? Dinner? Maybe a foot rub later?"

Her bottom lip starts to tremble. "*You* were the one at work all day. Shouldn't I be offering you those things?"

The sudden mood swing frightens me, but not him. He maintains his even-tempered nature and shakes his head. "It's work taking care of and *growing* our family. Just because you're not *currently* employed outside the house doesn't mean the job you're doing here isn't important or doesn't deserve recognition."

Tears fall to her cheeks as she cries out, "Why are you so perfect?!"

Oh my God, she's not going to need a doctor in the hospital. She's gonna need a priest, a bucket of holy water, and a Latin prayer to expel the evil that's currently flowing through her veins.

Archer maneuvers around the artsy mess on the floor, brushes away a tear, and leaves a kiss in its place. "I love you, babe." Afterwards he leans his fit figure further down to kiss her stomach. "And I love you, little man, even if you're making Mommy miserable."

Rainne quickly attempts to intervene on the action. "No, my Daddy!"

A stunned expression crosses his face before he directs it to Jaye. "When did this start?"

"Oh, you mean the hatred for the pending sibling?" She adjusts herself on the couch while I collect the crayons. "About a month ago."

"Why is this the first *I'm* hearing about it?"

"You leave early and work late."

The clip in her tone causes him to cringe. "Jaye you know-"

She lifts a hand to hush him. "Not in the mood to have that discussion."

Hurt hops into his eyes, yet he simply nods his understanding. "Alright. I'll take Rainne to play in her room…"

Once her husband disappears from earshot, I pin her in place with an incredulous stare. "Should we talk about that?"

Jaye shakes her head.

"You *know* this is what I do for a living."

"Technically, for a *living*, you read profile surveys for a dating site and pair people up to have sex."

"*Start* relationships," I promptly correct, "but you know what I meant. Relationships are my specialty. And you know I'm not going to just shove unsolicited advice down your throat like the average counselor. That's not who I am. That's not how I operate." Tucking my feet underneath me, I rest one arm on the edge of the couch cushion. "Rainne's response to a new child is *normal*. You may hate it, but often transitioning from only child to sharing your parents is a process. On the upside, she's begun earlier than some, which puts her ahead on the adjusting phase. She doesn't *hate* you or spending time with you or being around you. It's the opposite. She hates how she's no longer the only child around you, that you're no longer just *her mommy*. This shit started about a month ago when he started getting really active every day, right?"

Jaye slowly nods.

"Yeah, that was the moment *she* realized the baby is real and changes are about to happen…" My hand lands warmly on her leg. "Now, what's going on with the world's best hubby?"

162

She glowers. "Don't call him that."

"*You* call him that! You even bought him one of those tacky travel mugs that says it on there!"

"And didn't you get Gideon one that says number one best friend?"

"I did. And he hated it. Called it the worst Christmas gift until he opened the damn thing up to discover the bag of Cola Shaped Candy and monthly subscription to it."

He doesn't actually *use* the mug for coffee. He stores said candy in it so that his nasty little sweet tooth isn't public knowledge. Similar to the way he somehow manages to store tic tacs in my console, so it isn't constantly public knowledge that I eat as much salsa on my tacos as I do.

"Anyway," I drag the conversation back onto the right path, "what's wrong within the Cox household?"

Jaye buries one hand in her curls while the other rubs her stomach. "I've just…been feeling lonely and like a single parent lately. His corporate position requires him in the office early and at times to stay late, which isn't ideal when you're pregnant and have a toddler you need help with. Plus, he's had to attend happy hours to rub elbows and travel out of state for training. He cancels plans. Misses dinners. And family time. And *us* time. And I just…" she momentarily shuts her eyes, "miss him."

"Picking a fight and then banishing him from your presence *might not* be the best way to communicate that."

Her eyes narrow at me though a small smile touches her lips.

"What have I always told you two from the first time we met?"

"Communication is key."

"Exactly. That doesn't just apply to what happened to him in his past or what he feels is still weighing him down in his present. It's across the board. People have yet to develop mind reading powers, which is what makes verbal expression, no matter how difficult it may be, imperative."

She hums at the notion seconds prior to turning the topic to me. "So, when are *you* going to *verbally communicate* to Gideon that you're in love with him?"

"Oh…" My head quickly shakes. "We're not…Nope. Convo change."

Never said *I* was good at communicating. Just that it *needs* to happen in relationships. Which we are technically *not* in. Well, I mean a romantic one…And we're not. Just because we have sex doesn't mean we're together. Sex does not equate to commitment. That's a common misconception both genders make.

"Fine." Her quick surrender builds immediate worry. "Did you take that job Carly told you about?"

Not surprised by the shift from one serious subject to another, I flop my hands into my lap. "I have a phone interview scheduled next week. If they like me then they'll schedule an in person follow up."

Jaye's jaw drops. "What?! You actually sent in your résumé?!"

"I did."

"*And* agreed to a phone interview."

My finger creeps up to my lips. "I did…"

164

"That's amazing!" Her thrill threatens to grow a grin on my face. "You'll *love* that job. I mean...*really* love it. And they'll probably work with you to allow you to keep your hours at the clinic unaffected."

"That's the hope."

She gleefully claps. "What did Gideon say about the whole thing?"

"He doesn't know."

Her eyebrows dart down in perplexity.

"Haven't told him."

"Why...not?"

"He's been busy." I gnaw on the edge of my nail. "You know last weekend we had the charity thing in Connecticut, and then this week he had a meeting in California on Monday before having to fly back to Connecticut to try to seal the deal with the player they were hoping to recruit."

"He's been gone all week?"

"All. Week."

And it's been torture. Weird, mind-melting torture. Lying in his bed without him used to be no sweat but ever since things got...*physical* between us, it feels so empty when he's not there. I've been breaking out the big guns to survive this week. Bought him a brightly colored polka dotted pocket square I think he'll hate but pretend he loves. Rearranged his watches then pretended to hear the lecture I know he's going to give. Sprayed some cologne on a pillow and curled up against it. I even made sure to keep my phone charged, so I could prop it on the mattress like he was beside me while we watched *RoboCop* to sleep. He's texted me pictures and videos of BJ, which all prove the trip is worth it, while I've been sending him snaps of me raiding his fridge and enjoying his luxury bathtub. Strangely enough, this is the most glued to my phone I've ever been. He's grateful. And…if I'm completely honest with myself, I hate not being more active this way sooner.

"When does he get back?"

"He landed at noon," I inform.

"And…instead of being with *him* all afternoon, you're here with me…Why?"

"Because you're my other best friend and despite the demon inside of you, todavia te quiero."

"Which means?"

"I still love you."

"Mm. That's flimsy."

"But true."

Jaye tilts her head to the side.

"What? I do! I love you and spending time with you."

Her eyebrows lift in demand for the remainder of the sentence.

"Plus, he had a meeting, and then a date."

The glare she delivers sends chills to my core. "What the fuck do you mean he has a date?"

"Date número cinco."

166

"Thank you, Dora, The Date Explora." Her sarcastic retort warrants a smirk of approval from me. "You're still doing that ridiculous deal?!"

Slinking away from the conversation, I simply nod.

"Why, Lennox?! Why? Why? Why?"

"I have a good reason!"

"Why!" She practically shouts. "Why on earth would you continue this bullshit charade when it's *obvious* you both want each other? And before you try to sell me on that being a circumstantial conclusion, let me remind you that you had the best sex of your entire life this past weekend. With. *Him*."

It was the kind of sex they don't put in movies because it would have to change it from an R rating to the old school X rating. I've never been bent in so many positions or been required to eat so many tacos for fuel in my entire life. No wonder women are always requesting seconds and thirds with him. The man has perfected sex the same way he has his wardrobe.

"At first you were worried about being rejected, and then when that was put to rest, you were concerned about the effects on your friendship. Now that you're having sex, that's going to leave irrefutable changes for you two to deal with, so why wouldn't you just bite the bullet and go all in?"

"Because I'm afraid."

"Of?"

"Everything happening only because it's convenient."

Bafflement bursts into her eyes yet again.

167

"I'm convenient, Jaye. I already fit into his life, into his schedule. He doesn't have to fight to make things work with me because he's already spent so long making sure it does as his best friend. Being with me…doesn't require him to put himself out there or put forth effort into cultivating a relationship with someone *new.* I'm worried that…" the words taste like vinegar as they're regurgitated, "he's *settling* for me. That he can do better…should do better…but won't because I'm in the way. Because I'm already here. Because it's easier to just work with what you have than to find someone that sets your soul on fire. I know with these dates that he's at least getting to see there are better offers…better *matches* for him out there."

She tilts her head to the side and gives me a short, soft grin.

"I love Gideon. And I love him enough to let him go when he realizes he's ready for someone better."

Jaye leans over to pat the top of my head. "You're an idiot."

It's my turn to let my mouth become agape.

"But so is he. You'll both eventually figure out that you're perfect together and then be two idiots in love…Just like the movie with Mathew Perry and Salma Hayek."

"Fools Rush In is the movie you're referring to."

"Yeah, well, your movie would be called Idiots Who Are Taking Way Too Long to See The Obvious."

"That would be a *terrible* title for a movie."

"But *accurate.*"

I roll my eyes at her commentary to which she giggles.

For another few hours, I pass the time with the Cox family. We have burgers together per the demands of the pregnant woman, put together puzzles with Rainne, who provides us all with snuggles, and then have a subtle start to a counseling session where I simply open the door for them to get the real conversation going once I exit.

To my surprise, I don't receive a single text message from Gideon. I don't expect them *during* his dates because that's rude and would mean he's not giving the woman he agreed to be set up with all of his attention; however, he usually sends one when he's returned home, and I'm not there. Both reasonable reasons for his lack of reaching out has my stomach in knots. Either he's still on said date, meaning they're hitting it off, or things are going *extremely* well, and he's invited her back to his place to seal a different kinda deal.

The kind I was hoping I would be the last one he ever signed with.

God, Jaye is right.

I am an idiot.

At my apartment, I decide to distract myself to the best of my ability. The mention of the '90's romance sends me on a Mathew Perry path that starts with the aforementioned flick yet veers to the darker side with *The Whole Nine Yards*, inevitably leading me to *Die Hard* since, once you see Bruce Willis on screen, you *have to* see him in one of his more iconic moments. Throughout the films, I slip into a baggy white shirt, ditch my bra, banish my shorts, make a small grocery list, check emails, and fill in my schedule for the week after remembering I have a lady doc appointment on Thursday.

Not that I don't trust Gideon in that department. He literally tells me *and shows me* everything. I've seen his clean bill of health. I even recall the one time he was worried about crabs because he couldn't stop itching his crotch. Turns out he was just having an

169

allergic reaction to some fancy fucking soap he got when he was in France. Aside from him discussing his health habits, I know where he keeps his condom stash, though the fact it isn't beside the bed is something I do find fascinating. Most people keep it there for easy reach, but he keeps his in his closet, in his accessory dresser, in the drawer below his watches yet above his wallets. Like he never expects to need it in his own home. Like it's just one more thing he tucks on himself during his morning routine inspection.

My quoting along is unexpectedly interrupted by my phone vibrating on the end table. I leave one hand on the keyboard as if needing it to hold my place in the email and use the other to feel around behind me for the device.

The flashing text alert from Gideon has my heart trying to punch a hole in my chest.

What if this is it?

What if this is the text that turns us back in the direction we came?

What if this is the text that tells me I was right? That what happened was purely out of convenience because this woman, the woman *I* found him, is his perfect match.

Bile burns up my esophagus as another text from him flashes.

Fuck…It's worth *two* texts?

Yup.

Worst case scenario has arrived.

I shove down my sadness and swipe it open to reveal his messages.

OG: Where are you?

170

OG: Why are you not home?

My eyes dart around the apartment to reexamine my location.

Am I…Am I not?

Me: I…am?

OG: You're not.

Me: I am LITERALLY sitting on my couch watching Die Hard.

OG: FML. WITHOUT ME?!

His reaction receives a hearty laughter that I'm convinced he can hear regardless of our distance.

OG: Be there soon. Prepare to start it over.

I lightly snicker at the demand, take it back to the beginning, and leave it paused per his request.

Despite his decision to come over, my mind is still a battlefield of uncertainty. Sure, he was wondering why I wasn't at his place, but that doesn't mean the date didn't go well. It just means he wasn't willing to fuck her on the first night, or that maybe they went to her place instead because he has it in his mind we're roommates and having sex where I can't hear would be the more respectful choice. Or maybe he did take her back to his place, fucked her in the guest room, and then was just curious as to why I didn't meet him in the kitchen for a celebratory beer. Or maybe…just *maybe* he liked her but not enough to give up on whatever is building between us.

About forty-five minutes later, a sharp knocking interrupts my infamous '90's Girl Power mix that includes classics from The

Spice Girls, Christina, Britney, Shania, Mariah, and of course Ms. Whitney Houston. The laptop gets transferred to the cluttered coffee table, near a stack of medical journals, and I bounce over to the door to the rhythm of the song.

Gideon greets me with a wide grin upon it opening. "It sounds like *TRL* in here."

A smirk sneaks onto my face.

"Where's your 'We Love You Carson' sign?" His joke is proceeded with him squeezing by me, the plastic bags he's carrying accidentally brushing me in the process. "Or would you have gone *specific*? Maybe 'I heart B2K'?"

I shut and lock the door behind him. "Oh, like you would've passed up the opportunity to hold up a 'Britney Please Dump Justin For Me' sign?"

"Good rebuttal." Gideon chortles as he drops down onto my couch. "You in the mood for chicken or beef?"

Joining him on the couch, I try to contain my joy of the taco spread he's laying out. "One and one?"

"Figured." He pushes two foiled objects in my direction along with two small sides of salsa. "Beer?"

My nod is immediate.

Gideon grabs them from the other bag and begins to pop the tops. "Press play."

"Uh…how about a please?"

"How about a thank you for midnight tacos?"

I helplessly smirk at the counter. "Gracias."

A triumphant grin swiftly grows. "De nada."

"Though this feels like pity food," my mumble is accompanied by the starting of the movie.

"Pity food?" Gideon promptly inquires. "What the fuck does that mean?" The lack of immediate answering causes him to snatch the remote and return the movie to its still form. He nudges me with the side of his dress shoe to command my attention to his. As soon as our stares meet, he repeats, "What the fuck are you implying, Lenny?"

My mouth suddenly runs Sahara level of dry.

Gideon's brown gaze maintains its piercing projection, and I suddenly feel like there's a noose around my neck.

I can't just flat out tell him all my fears. That would make him fucking sprint for the hills. I know, I know, I preach to anyone who seeks my service the importance of communication, yet in my own life I tend to cut it short when it comes to the one person who probably could benefit from it the most. But how do you just blatantly tell someone you hate the idea of them loving anyone else? How do you word vomit feelings you've been keeping vaulted for…over a decade? I mean…*yeah*…I blurt out a bunch of shit, but most of it is meaningless or in good spirits. None of it has ever been life changing.

Except that one time I stopped Mateo from marrying a woman who was clearly cheating on him.

"Lenny."

"Pity because…" my words struggle to form the remainder of the sentence, "you…forgot to check in on me regarding dinner."

Gideon's gaze remains skeptical.

173

"Lucky for you, Jaye and Archer took mercy on me. I could've withered and died waiting on a text from you."

He finally rolls his eyes and returns to playing the movie.

Relief nestles itself comfortably on my shoulders.

"You know the fridge at home had *plenty* of food. You just hate having to cook for yourself."

"Why would I cook for myself when you and restaurants do it so much better?"

The corner of his lip kicks up seconds prior to him having a bite of his taco.

"And why are you hungry at midnight?" Against the nagging in my mind to not verify my earlier worries, I press on, wanting to rip it off like a Band-Aid. "Are these post bang munchies?"

Our eyes lock once more.

His lack of immediate response forces me to clamp my jaw shut tightly to prevent further accusations from spilling out. He casually chews on the food in his mouth making time suddenly slow down to an excruciatingly painful speed. Finally, he announces, "These are 'haven't eaten in over twelve hours' tacos."

Relief prepares to make an appearance yet is beaten by shock. "What? Why? Wasn't dinner on the date agenda?"

"It *was*, but the trip to the ER intervened."

"What?!"

Gideon nods and moves his taco towards his lips. My slapping of the back of his hand to stop the process has him

174

grousing, "Didn't you just hear me say I haven't eaten in twelve hours? Why are trying to starve me? Do you want *me* to *wither and die* in front of *you*?"

The teasing reference to my earlier statement gets a chuckle out of us both.

"Seriously, OG. What happened? Why were you at the ER, and why didn't you call me? *I'm* your emergency contact."

"It wasn't *for* me."

I throw my hands up in question.

"Gretchen, the twenty-nine-year old, Argentinian adrenaline junkie who looked like a *Sport's Illustrated* cover, but sounded like she had been smoking a pack a day for the past fifty years, decided that rather than go have dinner, we would *first* go visit some friends of hers who were performing motorcycle tricks on the outskirts of the city. I met her there. Learned her favorite recreational activity is to swim with sharks, and her *next* favorite is tricks on her bike. Conversation died there due to one of her pals encouraging her to perform. Regardless of being called a pussy for objecting to her doing that shit in front of me, you know since I'm a fucking stranger and have no idea what her skill levels actually are, I repeatedly voiced my concern, considering she hadn't done one in a couple weeks as a result of the trip she had been on for work. By the way, sports journalist was a good try," Gideon compliments. "Had it not been for what happened next, we probably would've had a lot to talk about."

There's no reluctance to inquire more details. "What happened next?"

"She did this move where her bike was up on one wheel and her legs were spread out wide into a V. Would've been impressive *and* sexy had she not landed poorly back on her seat."

My hands fly to my mouth.

"It was all…very graphic from that point forward. The crack of…something…was so loud I thought I was gonna puke. The paramedics had to be called, and she was rushed to the nearest hospital. I thought about bailing and letting her friends, the people who actually fucking knew her, be the ones to wait for results, but didn't wanna look like an uncaring asshole, so after much too much deliberation, I decided it was best to wait with them." He swipes his beer to take a well-deserved gulp. "I'm not sure on her condition other than she's alive. That's all they would give to those of us not family. I took that as my cue to leave and did."

"This definitely tops the worst date list…"

"Definitely tops the most *traumatic* list."

I reach for my beer bottle and apologize, "Sorry."

He offers me a kind smile.

For the second time against my better judgment, I poke around where I probably shouldn't. "Do you think…if you would've actually made it to dinner that…you two would've been a good fit?"

Gideon grabs his taco to return to devouring. "Probably not."

"Why?"

"Are you asking so dates six and seven can be altered to have a better chance at succeeding?"

"Yes."

"Thought you were good at this shit," he playfully taunts between bites, "thought you *knew me* and could 'find me a match' with no problem?"

176

"I didn't factor in *you* would be the problem."

"How am I the problem?!"

"Your shitty attitude!"

Lettuce falls from the taco as he tosses it back on top of the foil. "How the fuck do I have a shitty attitude? Am I or am I not showing up to these despite the fact I clearly have no interest in doing so?"

"They're probably picking up on that!"

"They're not."

"How do you know? How do you know that's not what you're projecting with your body language or snarky tone?"

He angles his body towards mine. "First off, I know what I'm throwing out there because I'm consciously giving this shit the best I've got out of respect for *you*. Do I have any fucking interest in being set up or listening to people ramble on about themselves without pausing to really listen to what I have to say? Not really. But I know *you* went through a helluva lot of effort to only pick the best matches you thought were worth risking your career for."

My lips press tightly together.

"Second of all, no matter how boring or annoying or painstakingly stupid I may find some of these women I have to engage in conversation with, I'd never let them know that because when you're on a date, those are the last emotions you want to feel. And if you went through the effort of putting yourself out there, those are damn sure the last emotions *I* wanna make you feel."

The sentiment is just as surprising as the ass-chewing he's skillfully executing.

177

"Lastly, has it occurred to you yet that maybe you're *not* good at matching people just because your strength lies within helping them maintain the matches they've already made?"

"Yes."

Gideon's body is blown backwards by my confession.

"And it's part of the reason I applied for a job as a relationship therapist this week."

Small part. The larger part, of course, being I would love to counsel people on better terms than my current office gig.

"You did?"

"Yeah. I actually have a phone interview on Tuesday."

"Why are you just now telling me this?" Consternation floods his expression. "Why didn't you tell me sooner? Why wasn't I the first person you told?"

"You've been busy!"

My response receives a hard glare.

"Between the whole thing with BJ and not really knowing if I was going to go through with sending my resume, it just didn't seem like something worth bringing up."

All of a sudden, Gideon does something unexpected. He leans in my direction, places his hands on my hips, and tugs me over until I'm straddling his suit-covered lap. I gasp at the change of position, yet he shifts backwards, eyes holding mine hostage.

"Lenny, your life…and what happens or what's happening with you, is *just* as important as mine." His thumbs gently stroke my hips. "Maybe I haven't always been the best at expressing that, but it

178

is. And I give a fuck about what's going on with you even in the middle of an insane work schedule. So, I'm *asking you* to please stop acting like one of us is an NBA star and the other a college freshman."

I can't stop the smile that sprouts.

"Are you hoping you get this job?"

"Kind of?" My shrug is innocent. "It would allow me to counsel full time, which I absolutely fucking miss."

"Why'd you really quit your job?"

The question sends my attention elsewhere.

His finger swiftly locates to my chin to force my stare back to his. "I know you. And you do *most* shit on a whim, like getting my Escalade washed or bringing in doughnut holes for the whole office, but that's not what that was. You quit for a reason. I wanna finally hear it. *All* of it."

After a long, deep exhale, I cave to his request. "I wasn't happy."

"Why?"

"They had me treating patients like numbers instead of people. It wasn't about how they were doing or adjusting or making progress. It was about how quickly can you get them on the schedule again and bring us in more money. It was a heartless operation based on exploiting the wealthy couple's desire to have at least one healthy aspect of their life." My stomach tightens as I add the final lines. "I also didn't like being sexually harassed. Mervin, the man whose practice it was, crossed a line the day I quit."

Gideon's entire body tenses underneath me.

"He came into my office to 'celebrate' the full roster of clients I had. Brought champagne. Spilled some on 'accident' on my shirt and offered to take it off for me to help it dry. When I said no and asked him to leave, he tried to unbutton it anyway. I may or may not have grabbed a pair of scissors from my office cup and threatened a testicle removal." A proud smile appears on my face. "He got the hint. Tried to give me a 'leaving bonus' as hush money for the incident. I took it and donated the cash to the clinic. Thought it would be nice for some good to come out of the bad."

"I think it's amazing how you're always concerned about others." His hands link at the small of my back. "But sometimes, Lenny, it's okay for others to be concerned about *you*."

"I didn't want you to worry. I mean, obviously, I'm fine."

"But I *wanna* worry," he firmly argues. "And I wanna be angry when someone disrespects you. And I wanna comfort you. I wanna do all these things that a..." the pause in his speech has me angling forward in hopefulness, "person you...trust does."

Ugh. Nice way of avoiding the boyfriend label.

"No more of that shit, okay? From this point forward, you talk to me about everything, the same way I talk to you about it. Agreed?"

"Agreed."

With, of course, the tiny exception of my undying love for you.

"Oh, and what was the guy's last name you used to work for? I think him and I need to have a little chat."

"No-huh." I quickly shake my head and wind my arms around the back of his neck. "You're not going to jail over some old asshole whose la esposa is sleeping with the pool boy, so he feels compelled to get even in his own work space."

He flips us around so that I'm on my back. "Fine, but I am going to voice my grievance about this shit."

"What else is new?"

Gideon momentarily glares before his hands inch up the edge of my t-shirt. "*How* I do it."

Intrigue has my heart beginning to race.

"Gonna eat this pussy until *I* feel better."

His fingers anchor onto the sides of my boy short underwear and start to tug them down. Once they're slipped past my ankles, he throws them over his shoulder and submerges himself between my thighs. The first lick of my pussy is agonizingly slow. My hands curl into fists at my side in objection. Gideon cocks a crooked grin, hooks his arms around my legs, and laps up the sticky sensation that's already leaking free. He maintains the leisurely speed. Whirls his tongue back and forth as if time is of the essence, and my orgasm of no importance. My muscles clench in anticipation of being touched, yet he avoids pleasing them by barely grazing his tongue around the entrance. Dissatisfaction effortlessly builds, and the evidence of it is grumble after grumble left to fester in my throat.

The moment he uses the tip of his tongue to lightly tease my clit, I can't restrain my complaints any longer. "Deja de atormentarme, papi..."

He rolls the tip of his nose against the area he's toying with before diverting his gaze up to me. "What's wrong, baby? Frustrated?"

I let my hooded stare narrow at him.

"Feeling...powerless?" His tongue steals another slow lick. "Like you know exactly what will make you feel better, yet can't make it happen because someone is in your way?"

"You're trying to teach me a lesson?"

"I'm *successfully* teaching you a lesson."

My pout is washed away by his lips delivering a deliciously hard suck to my clit. I whimper, dig my fingers into his hair, and concede, "I get it. I get it..."

He hums against the sensitive nub prior to shooting me another glance. "Do you?"

"You wanna *protect* me, and I haven't been letting you."

"I wanna *care for you* in ways you haven't been letting me."

The words leave my lips without consent. "Then do it, Gideon. Care for me."

He lets his eyes fall shut while his mouth lands back on my pussy. This time there's no soft touches or slow movements. His tongue dips deep inside. Repeatedly rolls upward. Strokes with voraciousness. Ravenous moans are released from both of us. Gideon's grip borderlines bruising, and I roughly grab a fist full of his hair to ride the tasty turbulence. Oscillating yanks are exchanged between desperate gasps for air. My thighs tremble in his clutches as my back bows off the couch, determined to not let us separate from one another until he's given the penance for his pain he deserves. An increase in his tongue's frenzy has my moans transforming into pants. I mumble out words in two different languages, eventually reaching a point of pleasure where I'm unable to create competent phrases at all. My nails scrape his scalp, a primal need to come clawing its way out of my system. He responds by grazing his teeth against my clit. The action is almost like a mirrored display of the pain to pleasure ratio I'm most likely distributing to him. His

182

audacious tongue abruptly presses flat against the aching area and applies so much pressure I have no choice but to detonate. Breathless screams spring from my throat as my entire body uncontrollably shakes. The loud, pleased growl ripped from Gideon's chest is followed by him laving his face in the orgasmic deluge.

I come and cry out in gratification.

I come and call out his name in content.

I come and capitulate to the request to care for me in previously unproclaimed ways.

He asked for all of me, and that's what I'm going to give him, even if it only ends up being temporary.

chapter nine

Gideon

Lenny props her elbow onto the aquamarine tablecloth and plops her face into her open palm. "Can't believe Christian's *married now.*" Her eyes peel away from where he's greeting guests at the reception and pin themselves back onto me. "*Married*, OG."

"Married," I playfully echo behind my glass of whiskey.

"We're talking *mar-ried.*"

"You say that like there's another type of married."

"There are several types of 'married', but that discussion is neither here nor there."

"Shouldn't it exactly be *here* since we're at a reception where you keep repeating the word married like you don't understand its meaning."

One of her free fingers runs around the rim of her cocktail glass. "He's *married.*"

"Yes...We were side by side trying not to laugh as they exchanged trite beach metaphors."

Which was fucking difficult. I'm not cynical, cold-hearted, or even opposed to you expressing how much your spouse-in-the-making means to you, however, when your vows sound like something out of a beach bum's guide to living the pothead life on the ocean's edge, I can only hold back my judgments for so long. I'm sure our wedding will have sports metaphors. Damn sure refuse to have vows that come out like taco recipes.

184

"You're not listening, OG." She drops her hand and slightly angles her body towards me. "Christian 'Can Barely Tie His Own Shoe' Cole is now *married*."

"Mmhm."

"To another living, breathing person."

"Who can also barely tie her own shoe."

Lenny lets the corners of her lips curl upward. "True…But come on, OG. This is the same guy we once saw drink beer out of an actual bottle while wearing nothing but a diaper that barely covered his crooked dick."

Jealousy gets the better of me. "How do you know his dick is crooked?"

"How do you *not* know?" She instantly counters. "Diaper disaster aside, he wasn't exactly cloak and dagger about his cock. You could pretty much just say the word, and it would appear like some unwanted genie there to curse you rather than make your dreams come true."

The walk down memory lane erases a portion of the possessiveness.

Previously, I never had the *right* to be this intolerant of hearing past romps or near romps or dick-related anything from her, but now that it's my cock *actively* in her life, I can righteously protest and then resolve my displeasure by providing her with some. Just because we don't have labels and haven't sat down to make everything official doesn't mean it's not.

Okay.

That's exactly what it means, but I'm working on it.

All I have to do is get through two more fucking dates. And the only reason I don't just call it all off is because she *insists* I finish our agreement. Fighting on the subject only stresses her out and fucks up her focus, which is the last thing she needs with a pending face-to-face interview this coming week. I can do this whole not really dating other people for two more rounds. I've got it all planned out. I'll meet them, apologize for putting them in the position they're in, and tell them the truth.

I'm in love with my best friend.

I'm going to ask her to marry me.

I'm sorry she put me on this dating site during one of our more irresponsible standoffs.

In an effort to wrap this shit up, I pushed Lenny to get them to me so I can wrap up this unusual period of time in our lives. Both dates had to be scheduled for the end of the coming week. I even took the initiative to use the email account she created to make contact, so she could focus on prepping for her interview. Originally, I was going to set up date six, who is only willing to sign her emails "L", on Monday since I'll be out of town Tuesday and Wednesday, but she said she already has solid plans for us on Thursday. Date seven, Natalie, is traveling until early Friday morning, so she suggested popping by my place to make me brunch once she lands. Perfect timing if you ask me. Lenny's interview is Friday morning, around the same time as my last moment in this dating faux pas, leaving Friday night to celebrate her new job *and* propose.

The second half of my plan seems…insane.

Very…*unlike me.*

Very impractical considering we've never even been on an official date.

But that's the thing.

186

We don't need to do some textbook bullshit.

We've already done it!

The lean on you during hard times. The make you laugh until you can't breathe. The long talks about absolutely fucking nothing, yet they contain the answers to everything. In retrospect. we've been dating for most of our friendship and only recently taken it to the next level. A level that I'd rather die on than ever leave. Lenny's letting me into much more than her abundance of boy shorts panties. She's finally opened up in ways that may make her feel vulnerable but make me feel like I'm the strongest motherfucker on Earth. I realized in our time together, she's always been the better listener, the better helper, the better...*partner*. It's always been my needs over hers. She has this habit of taking care of others that's hard to spot because her behavior appears so erratic, but after some reflection, I came to the conclusion that it's less random than it looks. Her goal is always to help others find, achieve, or maintain their happiness.

Sometimes that means ditching expensive steaks to slurp wing sauce off their fingers.

Sometimes that means subjecting yourself to an unwanted makeover.

And sometimes that means tricking your best friend into getting out of his own way to see how much you really love him.

"You okay?" Lenny questions, lifting her glass to her lips.

I blink away the clumps of thoughts to offer her a nod of reassurance. "I was just thinking."

She lifts her eyebrows for me to continue.

"People change, Lennox." My hand reaches over to take hers. "They grow up."

"He tried to drink from the champagne tower as she was pouring it."

"They *wise* up."

"He's had too many hits to the head for that to be true."

"They learn to focus on what brings them the most joy."

This time she bites on her index finger in response.

A sweet smile is accompanied by my removing of her appendage from her mouth. I lift it up to my lips to deliver a soft kiss. "Be good to your fingers, baby. My balls don't enjoy being groped by ones that feel like baby shark teeth."

Lenny rolls her eyes on a loud laugh.

"Want me to get you another drink?" I nod towards her nearly empty glass. "Probably gonna get myself a refill."

"Don't worry about it," she brushes off and stands. "I'm actually gonna go figure out how hard it is to pee in this thing and will swing by the bar afterwards."

I admire the tight, emerald green cocktail dress that is slightly off one shoulder yet down to mid bicep on the other side. It has a tight fit on her full chest and wide hips, along with a high slit that has me loving the fact I know she's not wearing anything underneath but hating that I have to wait hours before I can act upon it.

Lenny wiggles around uncomfortably forcing me to recall how much difficulty she had getting into her attire. "Why would you have a wedding *on the beach* but still require us to wear evening dresses?"

Leaning back in my seat, I merely offer her a shoulder shrug.

"It's horseshit," she grumbles, "and in protest, they'll be lucky if they see me in heels by the time they finally get around to our table."

Another smirk slides onto my face as I watch her stomp away in her black heels.

Once she's out of sight, I decide to do a lap of the star-studded event.

The issue *I* have with attending this wedding isn't the same one she voiced. What should be a beautiful, blessed, *personal* day has been made into a media circus spectacle that requires me to behave like a highly sought-after sports agent rather than just an old pal. I stroll through the venue, greeting players signed with our company, players who someday wish to be signed with us, and people who think my career is a joke in comparison to what they do. Never mind the time in law school I endured or the fact I helped build a lucrative company from the ground up. "Babysitting athletes' millions" should be considered an embarrassment.

Gotta love soirees like this…

My trek around the room eventually leads me to Christian, who has stopped making his tour to share a drink with what appears to be his groomsmen and Mick.

As soon as he sets eyes on me, he throws his massive linebacker arms in the air, splashing his drink on the man next to him. "Yeah! Lucas is in the house!" He gives me a solid pat to the shoulder. "So glad you could make it man!"

189

I give him a warm nod. "Me too. Never thought I'd see the day Christian 'Make 'Em Cry' Cole decided to let one woman lock him down for life."

"That's what I said!" His best man laughs.

My smile remains kind. "Congrats, again."

"Thanks, man!" Christian chuckles and proceeds to introduce me to the semi-circle of men gathered with him. "Tank, Newman, and Peters, this is Gideon Lucas, another old college bro and my agent who owns A+ Athletes with Mick."

We exchange handshakes along with polite greetings.

"Unlike Mick who just liked to enjoy the easy pussy that our parties always brought out back in the day, Lucas was on the team. Fullback." He looks upon me fondly. "Fucking good one, too."

Tank, the best man, promptly questions. "Why didn't you go pro?"

"Injured."

"Couldn't walk it off?" Peters pokes.

"Could barely walk at all," I inform, hands finding their way to my suit pockets.

"That when you decided to become an agent?" Newman inquires. "That whole can't do teach bullshit?"

"That'd be *coaching*." My correction is met with slightly drunken chuckles of agreement.

Mick unnecessarily comes to my defense. "Football wasn't the only sport Lucas loved, so coaching wouldn't have been the right call, anyway. A man who can spout out facts and figures of athletes

190

in every *major* sports league in America shouldn't be tied down to one sport."

"Just like Cole shouldn't be tied to any one piece of pussy," Tank loudly mocks on another round of laughs.

Christian shrugs it off though his stare locks onto someone in the distance. "Holy shit. Speaking of pussy, is that Long Legs Lennox?!"

Fuck, I forgot how much I hated that nickname.

Everyone's attention redirects to where my date is badly disco dancing with an elderly woman to "Love Shack" by the B52s.

"That's her," Mick quietly confirms.

He didn't care for it much either. While he wasn't ever interested in her the way I was, she was and *is* like having a younger sister he feels the need to protect.

"What the fuck is she doing here?" He rushes the sentence out. "You know, besides making a man wish he had seen her a few hours ago before he said yes so he could make her say yes all night."

My tone is tighter than my fists are curled. "It is part of my responsibility to remind you, Christian, that you *are* a public figure at a *very public* event with media eyes and ears everywhere." I lean slightly closer and drop my volume. "And as the man who is fortunate enough to have her in his bed every night, I suggest you watch your goddamn mouth before I end *both* of our careers."

Christian's expression transforms to one of shock while his groomsmen collectively decide it's necessary for another drink. Tank throws an arm around Christian to lead him away, however, before he's completely out of my vision, he offers me an unforeseen nod of admiration.

Can't make him stay true to his wife, but I can insure he doesn't disrespect mine.

And she is my wife.

With or without rings.

A ring will come soon.

Very soon.

I met with the jeweler yesterday morning for a consultation while Lenny was at the shelter for a morning shift. She thought I had a work meeting, which made her feel less guilty for not taking the entire day off to come out to South Haven Island for the wedding festivities. It was work in a way. There's so much shit to learn about picking the perfect ring. Cut. Clarity. Stone. Carrot. Vintage. Modern. Fuck, it was like having to learn stats on a brand-new fucking player you know nothing about other than you're required to sign him.

Mick clears his throat to grab my attention, but I leave my eyes on Lenny, not sure I trust Christian to keep his distance. "Did you just risk throwing away one of your top clients over a pass at our best friend?"

"No." Lenny's entire body starts to bobble back and forth like she's found the Holy Ghost in a southern Baptist church. "I risked throwing away one of my top clients for the love of my life."

The elderly female is soon joined by her husband who laughs at Lenny's wild movements yet tries to join in on them.

"Does she know?" Mick quietly questions.

"How ridiculous she looks? Probably not." A small shrug escapes me at the same time I chuckle at her antics. "Then again, there's a good chance she does and doesn't care…That's Lenny."

"I meant the being the love of your life part." Mick's comment causes me to grant him my attention. "Does she know *that*?"

Unsure of how to answer, I don't.

"Are you ever gonna fucking tell her?" He pushes. "You're already fucking *sleeping* with her, which by the way, thanks for letting *me* in on that little fact, congratulations."

My sneer is immediate. "It's not like that, Mick. Fucking her wasn't on my goddamn bucket list. I don't need praise for it."

"Was praising you getting your head out of your ass and *finally* making some progress with the only person you wanna be with on this entire planet."

Yet again uncertain of what to say, I remain silent.

"Tell her," he forcefully encourages. "Stop pussyfooting around like you're some asshole waiting on a better deal to knock on your door instead of signing the *perfect* one you were given. Stop wasting time. Close that deal. It is *literally* the most important one in your life."

"Mick!" Minnie squeaks, appearing out of nowhere. "Come on! I wanna go dance."

"Sweetheart, you know I hate dancing."

"But look at how much fun Lennox is having." She motions her head towards my date who is now doing the sprinkler with a group of children.

Mick offers jovial commentary. "Is she having a seizure?"

I helplessly chuckle at both her movements and his response.

193

"She's *having* fun!" Minnie takes his hand and slowly leads him towards the dance floor. "Besides, it's a wedding! There's always dancing at weddings."

Mick grumbles at her prior to throwing me a look over his shoulder. "Your ass better be coming with us."

After only a small hesitation I follow behind them, destination set on joining my better half. As soon as she spots me, she starts voguing, a clear throwback to our college dancing days. The small children gathered around her feet strike poses of dramatic fashions while I freeze in GQ worthy positions. We're eventually joined by the bride, Maisie, and her bridesmaids, who follow Lenny's anarchy by ditching their heels to dance more freely. Christian, along with the groomsmen, soon come over to partake in the fun. There's lots of laughter exchanged and lyrics shouted as opposed to sung.

The music transitions from the popular country song, "Shake My Boots Off" by Cooper Copeland to a classic that has both me and Lenny wildly smiling.

Everyone we're dancing beside sings the infamous lines to the opening while my date does what she always does when there's enough room.

She breaks into the infamous moves.

However, instead of waiting until much later in the song to join in, I immediately start on the first line of "Can't Touch This". Her eyes widen in surprise and delight alike. She continues to move around the space growing verbal praise for the moves she's busting in her cocktail dress.

When we reach the chorus again, Lenny hits me with a devilish grin. "Can't match this."

I laugh loudly at the parody of words and break out into the dance at her side. Parts of the wedding party try to figure out the fancy footwork while others just rap along. At the point the most infamous breakdown appears we all give our best Hammer impressions, most looking like drunken vacationers stumbling off a cruise ship.

Once the D.J. moves onto a slow song, many of the wedding party members disperse to grab refreshments.

"Should we get a drink?" Lenny inquires, hands planted on her hips as she blows damp curls out of her face. "Rest up for another round of showing Mick *yet again* who is ultimately the best dancer in our shared friendship?"

Despite the dull ache in my lower back, I extend my hand towards her and shake my head. "One more dance."

Lenny gives me a dramatically bashful look at the same time she drops her hand into mine. "Oh, my. To canción de boyband?" I pull her body against mine. "Does this one *count*? Technically, it's a country music song *featuring* a boyband."

"God, Your Mama, and Me" by Florida Georgia Line featuring The Backstreet Boys shamelessly pumps out of the speakers like its daring me to take the bait to engage in the pointless discussion.

My arms tightly wind around her waist. "Just shut up and dance."

She giggles and presses her cheek to my chest, arms matching my tangled position. I lower my face to rest my head against hers and let Mick's words mix with the message of the romantic melody.

Getting Lenny to agree to spend forever with me *is* the most important deal I will ever strike in my life. I'm prepared to negotiate until my dying days to get the "yes" I've always wanted. Just praying it doesn't take nearly that long.

chapter ten

Lennox

Why am I so nervous? Why do I feel as if I'm fourteen again trying to convince myself to tell Dave Carter that I think he's hot instead of a grown-ass woman who has simply chosen a cute, creative way to confess that she's in love with her best friend? He probably is already well aware of the fact. I mean…at this point how could he not be? We're inseparable. Sure, we were stuck together like glue before, but now we're also *sexually* plastered like two virgins who just stopped being virgins together. Our days used to frequently start and end with one another, yet after the wedding it seems we're on next level shit. Monday, he delivered me breakfast in bed followed by morning sex then shared it with me on Tuesday morning between conference calls, which he took in the kitchen via his Bluetooth rather than rushing into the office before catching his flight. He video chatted the following one, claiming he loves starting our days together and enjoys the laid-back nature I occasionally force him to take thanks to me rarely having to be at either job before ten. He promised we would start more of them at my pace if my new job allows for it. Ever since we started sleeping together a few weeks ago our days have passed with consistent texts, courtesy to my new habit of keeping my phone charged, while our nights are just as they've always been, except now we make out in the middle of a movie or bone on the couch during sports highlights. There's nothing left to do but make it all *official*, which is what he did on his end when he confessed after the wedding that he was canceling our previous deal because I was the only woman he wanted to spend his time with. I pushed *hard* for him to at least keep date number six. Told him, we could be exclusive *after* he went out with her, after he made sure she wasn't a good fit…He bitched. Griped. Moaned. Argued. Refused. And then, as he usually does when I pout for too long, he caved. Said he'd meet her, tell her he was crazy about someone else, and sorry for the inconvenience. He also made me deactivate the email account associated with the agreement to further reiterate the point he's completely done. It's been hard maintaining the secrecy that *I* am date number six. However, I will say I have put in quite a lot of pre-planning effort to make our first official date incredible.

Kristen greets me with a warm grin as I head towards Gideon's closed door. "Evening, Lennox!"

"Evening," I warmly state back.

"You look fantastic," she compliments, casually pointing to the neon yellow, halter top, summer dress I forced myself into.

Yeah. I put on *real* clothes for this thing. Not just basketball shorts and a tank top. His ass better appreciate it.

"Thanks."

"It's also fun to see lipstick *on* your lips instead of just pieces of paper." The tease is proceeded by a playful wink. "You can go on in. He's just making a video message."

"Yelling at his future self because he knows he's gonna be a stubborn dick about something?"

"Precisely."

I lightly giggle under my breath, knock twice on his door, and let myself in.

Gideon lowers the tablet he had been scolding into and lets his gaze grab the areas of my body it's obvious his hands want to. Once I've shut the door behind me, I saunter over to the desk, loving the way he licks his lips in hunger.

"Hey you." My butt braces itself against the edge of the furniture directly beside him. "Busy yelling or yelling busy?"

His glower is immediate. "You *know* that's not the saying."

"It is when it comes to you."

He rolls his eyes and relinquishes the hold on the device. "Are you just here to taunt me? Verbally and…" Gideon steals another glance at my long, bare legs. "*Physically.*"

A sly smirk spreads across my face. "I have no idea what you're talking about…"

"Is that so?" He turns in his leather chair to face me. "You have no recollection of the 'date' you made me keep this evening? Of the date that's stopping me from sending Kristen home early, bending you over my desk, and fucking you until security can hear your screams?"

I have to insert my index finger between my teeth to keep from moaning.

"Surely you remember since you snuck by before you went into work to drop me off an ice latte with a love note that was written in…chalk…?"

"It was chalk."

"Which, I gotta know *why* the fuck do you have chalk?"

"Couple's exercise at the shelter."

"Helping them keep score over whose turn it is to do which chore at home?" He chuckles at his own joke. "By the way, it's *always* time for you to do dishes."

"Excuse you. This is not a 1930's throwback sitcom. Men can cook and clean, too."

"Yeah, and as the man who has cooked and cleaned for the past fifteen years of our relationship, I'm saying you can *occasionally* do more than rinse out your cereal bowls."

"Hey! That's an improvement."

"It is," he swiftly agrees. "Kinda proud."

We laugh together at how ridiculous we sound and engage in a short, sweet kiss.

Afterwards, he states, "Thank you for the coffee by the way. It was really thoughtful. I would've sent a thank you text, but Mick pulled me into an impromptu meeting that ran dead into another. The day just got backlogged and before I realized it, you were knocking on my door."

"Everything okay?" I cautiously question.

Gideon gives my leg a gentle graze. "Not exactly. Looks like I may be working through the weekend."

"What else is new?"

He tries to hide his annoyance over the fact. "*At* the office instead of from home."

"What's going on?"

His mouth twitches in preparation of explaining yet abruptly stops. "Let's talk about it tomorrow night."

"OG-"

"Tomorrow night, Lennox," he firmly says. "You've got an interview in the morning. That's the only thing you need to be worried and focused on."

I smile sweetly at the sentiment.

There's really no need to worry. I either get it or I don't. I either go back to full-time counseling or continuing to help people find love. Okay, *hoping* I'm helping people find love and not just killing their dating spirit, like I did Gideon's.

"Wanna practice some of the tougher questions over dinner?"

"First of all, who would that really be fun for?"

He cracks a smile.

"Second of all, *no*, because you already have dinner plans."

"I'm not staying through an entire meal."

"OG-"

"No. I'm meeting this mystery woman, apologizing for wasting her gas, hell, maybe I'll even offer to reimburse her for it-"

"That borderlines instilling feelings of prostitution."

"Fair point." He nods. "Then just apologizing and leaving her money for her to enjoy a cocktail."

"That's *worse* not *better*."

His frustration flares. "Fuck. Whatever. I'll figure it out on the ride over. Regardless, I'm not staying. I'm saying sorry, and then coming home to my beautiful, taco loving girlfriend who is going to have to deal with eating Chinese tonight because we have fancy taco dinner plans *tomorrow*. You know my policy on back-to-back taco meals."

"Yes, and you know my love for breaking that policy."

More snickers are exchanged, and he keeps his smile bright. "And you know my love for you…"

Breathing suddenly becomes impossible.

Oh shit, should I say it back?

Was that an "I love you" or something similar used to gauge the situation, like "I love spending time with you" bullshit? Why am I so bad at reading *his cues* but an expert on everyone else?

Gideon softens his gaze. "Were you just stopping by to make sure I was going on the non-date, date or was there something else?"

Seeing the perfect opportunity for the announcement, I take it. "Oh, you're going on the date. And it's going to be a date, date because it's with *me*."

A dumbfounded expression instantaneously appears.

"*I'm* date number six."

His response doesn't change.

"I'm L, the bi-racial life coach, who loves golf."

"You hate golf."

"I love *put-put*, which is a golf affiliate."

"It isn't."

"It is."

202

"There's no professional put-put team."

My hand flies into the air to hush him. "Soy yo. I spun the truth as best as I could to keep it a secret, but it's me." I give him a small shrug. "I've kinda been planning it to be from the beginning."

The bewildered stare returns.

"Carly thought it would be a good way to test the idea of *us* out...you know if you didn't find a match before then."

His jaw cracks.

"This is basically our first official date, so I couldn't let you fucking cancel."

My choice to cuss causes him to chuckle. "What do you have in mind?"

"Well-"

"Can't Touch This" starts blaring throughout the room alerting me that I've got a phone call requesting my attention.

I dig in the purse dangling from my shoulder, silently cursing that it's flooded with junk. This is why I prefer pants or shorts with pockets. I don't have to play hide and seek with my cell, a game that it is currently winning.

Once I finally find it, I see Jaye's name and picture flash on my screen, which instills an unusual feeling of dread.

Gideon immediately notices. "What's wrong?"

"I don't know," I promptly reply. "Jaye's calling, and she *never* calls. She abides by simply policy to text me first unless it's an emergency." He barely has time to nod his understanding before I'm rushing to answer. "Hello?"

She groans loudly into the device. "Help. Me."

"What?! What do you need?!"

"Labor," Jaye grumbles again. "Gone into labor..."

"What!?!"

"Why are you shouting?" Gideon questions. "Is she okay?"

"Need," there's another pause proceeded by more unhappy groaning, "a ride."

Instead of asking the million questions racing through my mind, I instantly agree, "On it. We're on our way! We'll be there ASAP."

"Where are we going?" Gideon cautiously asks.

"To take Jaye to the hospital."

"Why?"

"She's in labor."

His eyes widen, but he quickly breaks free from the shock to collect his essentials.

After speeding across town, saying a silent thank you prayer that Gideon drove his SUV to work today, and relocating my very miserable best friend from her empty house to a bustling hospital, I have managed to gather one very important thing.

The run up to giving birth is a nightmare.

Jaye shifts around in the bed that looks more like a trap she's stuck in than a place of comfort. "Why is this baby in such a rush to get out of me?!"

"Isn't that a good thing?" Gideon carelessly questions.

Her stare becomes Samurai sword sharp.

"Don't poke the bear, OG," I quiet whisper.

"I am not a bear!" Jaye cries before roaring in pain.

That sound would imply otherwise.

While she has been, "does anyone know a good preacher" scary during this pregnancy, today, due to the situation at hand, she has reached the "may God have mercy on all our souls" level of terrifying. Turns out the worst way to go into labor is when you're home alone with your beloved father on duty, your mother at the movies with your daughter, and your husband nowhere to be found. Thankfully, I answered when she called, otherwise there would've been a chance she would've been brought here in an Uber.

"Breathe," my encouragement receives her scowl.

"Don't *taunt* her…."

Gideon and I exchange glares again.

Neither of us are comfortable in this situation. Him even less than me. I haven't ever been around someone when they were in labor. I've always been lucky enough to where I didn't have to show up until I got the magical "You're an Aunt" phone call. Had I been forced to do this in the past, pretty sure I would've opted for the five-year IUD rather than the three year one in the arm.

A soft sob out of my best female friend breaks our standoff. "I don't wanna do this alone."

I spring to my feet and over to her bedside. Taking her hand in my mine, I swear, "You're not alone, Jaye. Estoy aquí. Gideon's here. We will *not* leave you until your husband gets here or one of the nurses gets physical and drags us out."

Gideon crosses over to join her other side. "And good luck to the one that tries that method. May not be a fullback any more, but I'm still built like one."

Deliciously so.

My bottom lip slips between my teeth as sexual thoughts start to trample their way to the front of my mind.

He catches on and a similar, sly smirk slides onto his expression.

Unfortunately, our flirting only frustrates Jaye further. "Ugh. Would you stop fucking flirting while I'm waiting for a *child* to come out of my vagina?!"

The word vagina makes my boyfriend squeamish.

God, I can't believe I get to call him that.

"Just so you both know, flirting leads to kissing, kissing leads to sex, sex leads to this pain, misery, and *murder* if my husband doesn't answer his goddamn phone!"

Politely, I volunteer, "I'll try him again."

"Why don't *I* try him while you wait with her?"

Gideon's swift suggestion causes me to sneer.

She may be my best friend, but she's clearly been taken over by an alien host right now, and I'm not sure I'll survive on my own.

206

All of a sudden, Nurse Annabelle cheerfully walks into the room. "How are things in here?"

"Hell." Jaye unleashes another deep groan of discomfort. "God, the contractions are getting worse."

The less than five-foot, dark haired nurse, who looks more like she should work in Santa's Workshop than the hospital, approaches the foot of the bed to inspect the situation. However, her choice in not saying anything sends panic through my system almost as instantly as it does Jaye's.

"Everything okay?" My best friend's voice does its best not to shake.

Nurse Annabelle keeps her practiced, plastered polite demeanor. "I'm gonna go ahead and give Dr. Raymond a phone call to come down here. Okay?"

Jaye's eyes enlarge, and the tears in them are caught by the shitty lighting. "Okay..."

The woman makes her exit as does Gideon, more determined than before to get a hold of Archer.

"That's not good," she confesses under her breath. "They only get the doctor when something is *wrong*."

"Or...when you're ready to deliver, right?"

Her chin trembles in fear, yet she nods through it. "Right..."

But then that's still something that's terribly wrong because what woman wants to deliver a baby without her husband *present*?

I give Jaye's hand a loving squeeze.

She sniffles against her own volition and squeezes back. "Distract me, please."

"Gladly." My cheerful agreement gets us both to smile. "You know, I prefer the movie *9 Months* to *Knocked Up* and not just because Hugh Grant was in ways like the English Brad Pitt of the '90s."

A small smile creeps onto her expression.

"Not sure if it's my *favorite* Hugh Grant movie though. It's definitely up there. Hugh Grant was like chick flick catnip back then. He's probably partially responsible for many women's English accent obsession in this country. Did you ever watch *Two Weeks Notice* or *Love Actually*? It's like *come on*. Who can resist that smile tied to the fancy way he talks?"

For the first time since we picked her up, she actually laughs. "Not sure I thought he was *that* cute."

"Fine, but you agree. He's a '90's classic chick flick leading man."

"He was definitely that..."

Our conversation, thankfully, gets interrupted by the man of the hour. Archer rushes over to the opposite side of the bed from me and embraces his wife tightly. "I'm here! I'm here!"

She melts into his arms and begins to bawl. "Where the hell have you been?"

"Was in a meeting," he confesses, holding her tighter. "I'm so sorry, babe. So. So. Sorry."

My eyes dart over to where Gideon is leaning against the wall beside the doorframe.

If we were to have kids, not that I'm in any kind of rush or *need* to have them pop out of my pussy, part of me fears this exact scenario. I would probably respond just like Jaye. I'd be livid. Sad. Emotional. I would question the same thing I used to about OG. Is *work* the most important thing in his life?

Archer pulls back to meet her gaze. "I wasn't expecting you to go into labor for another couple of weeks, otherwise I would've had my phone right in front of me."

Jaye nods as he brushes away the fallen tears.

He tosses me a look of gratitude. "Thank you for bringing her and for being here."

"Of course."

His eyes fall back to his wife. "Your mother knows, and she's going to keep Rainne until we're ready for her to come up to meet her little brother."

There's a small knock on the frame followed by Dr. Raymond entering the room. "Evening. You must be the father."

"Archer," he extends his hand towards male, "and I'm also the *husband*."

"Good." Dr. Raymond nods. "Seems you might be here just in time."

"Delivery?" I hopefully question.

The dark-skinned bald male gives me a warm look. "That's something I need to discuss with Jaye and Archer in private. All non-family members should now relocate to the waiting room."

Hiding my disappointment over not receiving a response is difficult. "Oh…"

209

"We can do that," Gideon interjects. "We can wait out there, if that's what you guys want. Or we can go home and come back tomorrow or whenever."

Jaye shoots me a pleading look. "Do you guys mind waiting? You were so incredible getting me here and waiting with me for Archer. I would love to introduce our son to his Godparents sooner rather than later."

"Holy shit, we're Godparents?!" I squeak.

"We were going to sit down and officially ask you two over dinner next week, but…" She spans her hand across her body.

"We'll stay." Gideon's voice is firm, yet filled with awe.

"Thank you," Archer states to me and then him.

I give Jaye a sweet kiss on the forehead and stroll around to link hands with Gideon.

We direct ourselves to the practically vacant waiting room, choosing seats in the furthest corner. It doesn't take long before shock over the situation shoves us both backwards in our chairs. While I thought the events leading up to our first date were a bit un-ideal, I never pictured it would unfold this…poorly.

Where's the chick flick script writers like John Hughes, Richard Curtis, Michael Elliot, Gina Prince-Bythewood or Amy Heckerling when you need them?

Slumping down in the seat, I let my head hit the back of it as I sigh, "*This* has to be the worst date you've ever had. We're talking of *all time*."

Gideon's growing grin catches my attention out of the corner of my eye. "Of all time? You mean even worse than the time back in college when that Allie chick blew cheeseburger chunks all over my lap because she was too hungover to be on said date but thought she could *Varsity Blues* her way to the NFL with me?"

The gagging is instant. "God, I forgot about her."

"How could you? Thanks to that little stunt the apartment smelled like old tequila and dog shit for over a week."

"She's the reason you almost went *vegan*."

"Vegetarian," he corrects with a sharp point of the finger. "And yeah, that would've fucked up my career choice severely." The memory of a fallen dream surprisingly doesn't cause a longing gaze to blossom like it's been known to. "*She* was the worst date I ever had, period, though nearly having a woman die on you is a close second. As for worst *first* dates?" Gideon shrugs. "This one really isn't that terrible."

"Not that terrible?" My body darts upward and spins to completely face him. "Our date was hijacked by my pregnant best friend who then proceeded to have a Dr. Jekyll, Mr. Hyde response to *everything* that was said to her. We've spent three hours in her hospital room where she nearly broke my hand and attempted to shatter the spirit of what has to be the world's *happiest* nurse, only to be kicked out of the room by Dr. Crabby seconds prior to being informed we're *Godparents*. How is any of that *not that terrible?*"

"You mean aside from the obvious fact I'm doing it all with you?"

Being torn between swooning and dramatically dry heaving has my face scrunching in contemplation.

"Nothing *awful* is happening, Lenny. We helped a friend in need. We stuck by said friend when she was probably the most scared she's ever been in her life. We were then granted reprieve by

211

being dismissed before bad news could dampen the day *and* rewarded for our commitment to them as a couple."

I can't stop myself from sneering. "When did we switch places? When did you suddenly start looking for the *good* in the ugly?"

"Probably when you turned the dick Mick drew on my cast into a cartoon man with a fucked-up nose." Gideon's hand falls to my thigh. "Just because I don't always point it out, doesn't mean I don't see it." His thumb gives the area a gentle caress. "You've taught me so much and made me a better person, baby. Never doubt that."

Okay maybe I *don't* need a professional screenplay writer to fix this hot mess.

Maybe this hot mess is *perfect* for us.

"Can I ask what you actually had planned?" He briefly pauses. "Or maybe I should ask, *did* you actually have something planned? Were you just gonna wing it?"

The shift from sentimental to the original subject at hand has my shoulders slumping again. "I made us plans."

"*Real* plans or you doodled pictures of shot glasses and it inspired you to wanna go do bar trivia?"

"You *love* when we play bar trivia!"

Gideon lightly laughs. "Wasn't saying I didn't."

I push past the urge to point out how he loves my spontaneous side to inform, "I made *real* plans. Like ones where I had to make a reservation type of plans."

His eyebrows jump to the ceiling.

"I booked us tickets to this beer tasting thing. Runt's is rolling out new seasonal flavors this fall, and this was like their premarket taste test. We'd tour the facility, try the new beers, and then at the end there is this bratwurst buffet dinner."

"You hate bratwurst."

"I hate the weird white shit they put on top for decoration."

"*Sauerkraut.*"

"Yeah. That shit."

Another chuckle bounces his chest. "You really had that booked for us?"

"I did!" I hastily nod. "And tickets weren't cheap or easy either. It was like the first hundred people only. I stayed up until midnight just staring at the screen waiting for them to go live."

"That's commitment."

"I wanted *our* first fecha to be memorable."

"Lenny, every moment with you is memorable."

His sappy statement sends more sadness to the pit of my stomach.

This is so not what I wanted for tonight. This is absolutely *not* how I wanted to make our relationship "official". Or was it official when we first slept together? Or was it actually official when we kissed that night in his kitchen? Who gets to dub what day was the day that put us on this path? This brand new, built years ago yet just now being taken, path?

213

An idea pops into my mind, and I spring onto my feet. "We're not calling this a terrible first date!"

"You're the only one calling it that."

"I meant…" I mockingly bob my head at him, "we are going to enjoy what's left of our first date while we're waiting for our Godson to be born."

He cocks an eyebrow in question.

"Give me like five minutes."

"A normal person's five minutes or a Lenny's five minutes?"

"Lenny's."

"So closer to twelve?"

"Exactly."

We both snicker at the exchange before I disappear from view.

Gathering the items for the first part of my plan is easy, however, the folding process of the second half takes longer than anticipated due primarily to the fact I can't recall the best technique to create the desired object. Once I finally have it, I increase the speed of execution and rush back to my date.

Upon my arrival, Gideon tucks his phone back out of sight, unconsciously reminding me of the terrible work day he had yet hasn't talked about.

I clutch the items closer to my chest. "Do you need to be working?"

"Instead of...," his index finger flails my direction, "whatever this is? Absolutely not."

"OG-"

"No."

"Gideon-"

"*Lennox*, work can wait. Now, what the hell is all that?"

After a moment more of reluctance, I set down the sodas, snacks, and folded paper footballs on the table closest to us. "*This* is our date. Dinner. Drinks. And football."

A hand flies to his chest. "You know the way to this man's heart."

"Most of the time," I teasingly agree. "Sometimes I like to off road it just to watch that vein in your head pop."

"You know, I fucking *know* that and still feed into your bullshit when you do."

"Yeah!" My giggles are followed by me sitting back down and pulling the table closer. "It's hysterical. It's like a dog having to chase a tennis ball. It's instinctual."

"Fuck you."

"Fuck you, too."

We lean over and warmly press our mouths together. Not opposed to making out in the waiting room, but not wanting to get kicked out before Jaye gives birth, we engage in the kiss for under a minute.

Our previously lost date steers itself back on course. The two of us open our sodas, toast, and begin discussing the rules of our paper football tournament. We set the scoring system. Agree to the regulations. Decide on a time limit along with a prize for the winner.

I allow Gideon to fling his folded triangle piece of paper first, insisting, since I arranged the date, the date I invited should go first. Unfortunately, he flicks a perfect goal, and I'm left regretting my polite decision knowing I need to stay steady with his score or prepare myself to lose already. Back and forth, we take turns firing the objects to their destinations. Two people in the waiting area frown when we laugh too hard or trash talk too loud over missed plays while the others casually watch as if thankful for something more than their phones to pay attention to. We devour our chips and candy bars between our turns. Crinkle the garbage beside one another's ears to distract their shot. Attempt to bury our bellowed chuckles behind our balled fists.

I block Gideon's line of vision with my cheesy palm to which he grumbles, "You're gonna get that shit in my pores. Move."

My hand falls on a snicker. "You have to know how unmanly that sounds."

"Real men have no shame when it comes to giving a fuck about their hygiene." He launches the projectile into the air, it lands on the very edge of the coffee table goal line. "Yes! We are now officially tied!"

"Damn it."

His beam brightens at the same time he reaches for his half-emptied bottle of Dr. Pepper. "You know these are my favorite games to watch."

"Equally matched opponents?"

"Exactly."

Can't believe I'm starting to believe we're equally matched in other ways.

I offer him a small smile. "Which one of us is going to teach our Godson about football?"

"Shouldn't that be a *joint* venture?" The proposed idea is proceeded by disbelief flooding his expression. "Still can't believe they picked *us*. *You* I can understand. You're one of Jaye's best friends. You're close. You're always there when her and Archer need...direction. You've impacted their lives in multiple positive ways. It makes sense. But me? I'm just the tag along to shit."

"You and Archer hang out."

"Yeah, when we're all together at cookouts or grabbing dinner. Sometimes we bond when we're on the same team during game nights, but we never hang out *alone*. We're not *those* friends."

"Archer doesn't have many of *those* friends. And truthfully, the fact he hangs out with you at all, even if it is just in group settings, speaks volumes. There's a lot of trust issues there with what happened to him in the military, so him feeling comfortable around you to carry on a personal conversation is incredible."

A hint of redness tints his cheeks.

"Besides, they picked *us* because we're a packaged deal."

"Oh yeah?"

"Yeah. We always have been. It's just now our deal includes a little bit of kissing..." I let my finger creep down the front of his dress shirt.

He inches his mouth closer to mine. "*A lot* of kissing."

My tongue snakes out to tease his top lip with a single stroke. "A little bit of foreplay…"

His groan is heavy. "*A lot* of foreplay."

"And a little bit more time on our knees."

"*Not enough* time on our knees." The declaration is stated prior to him taking a small nip of my bottom lip. "Have I mentioned us being together is my favorite deal of all time?"

I prepare to use the response to the sentimental statement as my big I love you when Archer's voice interrupts, "We have a boy."

Our faces snap to where he's approaching.

"We have a beautiful, healthy baby boy."

"Congrats!" I squeak, springing onto my feet and embracing him in a tight hug. "I'm so happy for you!"

He gives me a gentle pat in return.

Afterwards, I break apart for him and Gideon to exchange a much shorter similar action.

Archer's weary face does its best to remain cheerful. "Jaye had to have an emergency C-section. She had a prolapsed cord, so they needed to move immediately to insure her safety and our son's."

My voice drops to one of more concern. "Is she okay?"

"Yes…Thank God." He runs a hand through his hair. "But, she's refusing to get some rest until the two of you meet our boy."

"You sure you wanna do that now?" Gideon questions.

"We're sure." He gives my boyfriend a good pat on the arm. "Then you two can get out of here and get some rest as well."

We quickly collect our trash, dispose of it, make a pit stop to clean our hands, and follow Archer to where they relocated Jaye.

The moment we enter her room there is an air of calmness that's immediately infectious.

She has to force herself to look away from the bundled baby boy in her arms. "Hey…"

"Hey…" We greet back in unison.

Archer abandons us to sit on the edge of his wife's bed. He kisses her and then kisses his new son like he's uncertain they're both real.

"We would like you both to meet your Godson, Alexander Charles Cox."

I can hardly contain my joy. "Is he named after what I think he's named after?!"

Jaye giggles during her nod.

"What's he named after?" Gideon quickly questions.

"A children's book," Archer answers with pride. "One of her favorites of all time."

"Wait," my boyfriend curiously interjects, "are you referring to *Alexander and the Terrible No Good Very Bad Day*?"

The three of us nod in unison.

A warm chuckle escapes him. "I remember that book. It had a good message at the end of it."

"Exactly," Jaye agrees, kissing her son sweetly on his forehead. "Everyone has problems. You can't run from them. And sometimes just a line of reassurance from a loved one, just a little compassion or reminder that you're not alone, can make all the difference." Her eyes soar to her husband who has tears forming in his.

Remembering the sweetness of their story and having it now bonded through a new baby threatens to make me cry.

Ugh.

Total chick moment right now.

"Wanna hold him?" Jaye softly offers.

"Oooo," I cringe uncomfortably. "That...that...that seems like a risky idea at the moment. Shouldn't I wait until his like baby balance kicks in or something?"

She shakes her head at me slowly.

"Is that not a thing?"

Her smile is sweet. "Not exactly."

"It's easy," Archer reassures. "It's like cradling a football."

"Bad analogy," Gideon jokes. "She *drops* footballs."

"F you, I do not."

"Look at that, Alexander. Aunt Len Len is already censoring herself for you," Jaye teases.

Well, glad she's in a better mood...I wanna point out that Alexander was crabby in the book, which is probably why he was *making* her cranky. He was just trying to live up to his namesake.

There's no point in trying to deny the offering a second time. Jaye carefully extends her newborn to me insisting with a stern look that I hold him. I do everything in my power to handle him as gingerly as possible. He's larger than I expected but lighter than he looks. His green eyes that match his father's glow at the mere sight of me.

My heart beats faster in adoration.

Pumps harder preparing to protect him from anyone who would dare to hurt him.

Swells in gratitude for being trusted with helping love such a gift.

Gideon unexpectedly places one hand on my waist while using the other to gently touch the child's face. "Hey, Alexander."

The baby's eyes shift to his and grow wide.

"I know. He's a big dude." My playful comment causes Gideon to chuckle. "But he'll cover you and your dad just like he's always covered me. He's a fullback for *life* rather than just football."

Alexander's full lips twitch in what I like to think is a smile.

"Why don't we get you back to Mom and Dad, angelito? We'll come by again tomorrow to see you." I divert my gaze up to Gideon. "If that's okay with you."

"Of course," he warmly states. "If that's okay with Mom and Dad..."

We both look back at the couple who are curled together, expressions exhausted yet overflowing with love.

"You are welcomed to come spend time with your new nephew and big sister niece anytime," Jaye announces on a yawn.

I carefully shift Alexander back over to Archer who decides he needs to hold him for a bit. Gideon and I give our love one last time before exiting the room. Our car ride back to his office is mainly filled with loving silence.

It's more than obvious both of our emotions have surged over such a momentous event. Hell, over such a momentous *day*. In less than twelve hours we went from friends who happen to be fucking to friends who are dating to friends who are dating and also *Godparents*. Talk about going big or going home.

After I agree to follow him to his mansion, I drive myself over to his place knowing the only reason we're not carpooling is because I need to leave fuck early to get ready for my interview in the morning.

The two of us are barely across the threshold when his mouth captures mine. Its feverish plunge receives a pleased sigh followed by my hands flying to undo his tie. Our actions increase in frenzy during our pursuit to the closest room, leaving clothes behind like a trail of breadcrumbs in some filthy fairytale.

His tongue twists and tangles.

His touch caresses and claws.

His thirst is quenched and immediately unquenched.

We tumble onto the couch, barely parting in the process. Straddling him isn't even a choice at this point. It's grown into something darker. Needier. More urgent and uncontrolled. I can't command my body to decrease its crazed speed nor can I demand it

222

slow down to enjoy the delicious descent onto his dick. With my grip anchored into the back of his neck, I impetuously sink until I know he can't go in any further. Groans of approval barely have time to do more than fester in the back of his throat. My knees dig into the cold leather of the couch for leverage as I lift myself back to the tip to repeat the submerging action. His hands cup my ass roughly to provide assistance. They firmly flex to guide me by the globes to the ravenous rate we're both drawn to. Up and down, and up and down my body bounces like my knees are on springs. The continuous acceleration has my pussy rapidly pulsing, grasping for more friction. Begging for deeper penetration. Pleading to pull the impending orgasm out of the shadows. I moan his beloved mixture of English and Spanish against his lips only to receive bites in return. Each word that slips off my tongue is ravished by his or cut short by his teeth nibbling away the sentence.

Nibbling away my sanity.

To my surprise, Gideon doesn't take over the situation with harsh thrust after thrust. Instead, he allows me to brazenly buck and recklessly roll every which direction I need in order to feed the wet, hot burn. I press myself against him so tightly there's a twinge of pain from my hard nipples being crushed. The small salacious ache makes me wetter, and Gideon's cock swells the second it notices.

His mouth locates to the crook of my neck where he scrapes his teeth along my lifeline.

"Oh, Dios mío." I squeeze my eyes shut, shuddering through the sensation. "Si, Papi. Si…"

Gideon's growl is more feral than I'm accustomed to. "Fuck, yes. Say that shit again."

When there's a delay in my fulfilling the demand, he delivers a swift swat to my ass to steal it out of me. "Si, Papi."

"That's right," he sexually grumbles against my skin. "I'm your fuckin' Papi, baby." Another quick spank lands on the area that's still sore from the last one. "Your fucking perfect match." He smacks me once again, this time receiving a mewl for more. "Your fucking everything."

The proclamation attached to the popping causes me to explode. My pussy throbs while my body temerariously thrashes. Screams cascade over us as wetness from my orgasm does the same to his nuts. Gideon releases a holler of my name seconds before searing ropes of cum splash inside of me. Our releases aggressively amalgamate like they're trying to permanently cement us together.

We've been bonded by our souls much longer than we have been by our bodies.

I used to think just most of Gideon was enough. That I could survive on our unbreakable friendship alone.

I was wrong.

I was so beautifully wrong.

There's an unfathomable sense of completion in my life since we've shared this part of ourselves. And it's a completion I have no doubt I will get to experience for the rest of my existence.

chapter eleven

Gideon

Lenny's phone alarm shrieks from the nightstand beside her.

She stretches over to shut it off, yet remains in bed primarily due to my arm keeping her pinned in place. "Buenas mañanas, baby."

Her Spanish registers to my lower brain first. I lazily roll my stirring cock along the crack of her ass and nuzzle my scruff against her neck. "It will be a *great* morning in just a couple minutes."

Lenny tosses me an inquisitive look over her shoulder. "Have you forgotten what today is?"

Our gazes meet, and my hand snakes over to softly stroke her side. "Of course not."

"Then you know I have to leave."

"Yes, but everyone knows the best way to go into an interview is as relaxed as possible."

"And you really think I have time for that?"

"I'll make it quick." I wink.

She giggles and wiggles. "Not *too* quick. I didn't set my alarm early to have to *fake* an orgasm before the interview."

A mixture of mirth and joy thrum through my stare. "First of all, you'll *never* have to fake an orgasm again. You'll always get one from me whether it takes me two minutes or two hours."

Lenny helplessly whimpers.

"Second of all, did *you*, Lenny 'Five Minutes Late Is Close Enough' Marston, actually set an alarm *early*?"

She slowly nods. "Your fault."

"My fault?"

"Do you not see the better adult I've become? Using calendars and charging my phone and now...*early* alarms!" Her faked outrage is spoken with a smirk. "I mean what's next? Taking vitamins?"

"You really should be taking vitamins."

Her eye roll is immediate.

"I'll get you the gummy ones at the store later, so you think you're eating candy instead." My hand glides off her side and onto my cock, positioning it against her entrance. "But for now, how about we start your day with a little vitamin D?" I rub the head of my dick up and down between her lips. "Warm up those vocal chords with a few screams of my name?"

Lenny's breath hitches at the idea, and I push the tip inside just enough to tease her. Pouty puffs are set free, yet a smug smirk crawls onto my face.

It's intoxicating to know the one person you want like an antidote to a fatal disease you didn't know you had wants you just as fucking badly.

Each shallow rock results in wetness whirling around my cock, whispering for me to come in a little deeper.

Push a little harder.

Make her arch a little more.

The erotic taunting gets the better of me before I can stop it. In a flawless movement, I lift Lenny's leg up and thrust sharply inside. Her head hits the pillow at the same time her body bows backwards to meet the blow. A moan so soft it sounds more like a spiritual hymn than a moan hypnotizes my hips into moving at a much slower pace than either of us are used to. Our unusual change in speed tempts me to shut my eyes and get lost in the scorching sea my cock is being bathed in, but Lenny's weak whimpers win my attention. I intensely watch the manner in which ripples of pleasure spread throughout her system. Observe the beautiful way her full tits bounce each time our bodies crash. Groan at her bottom lip trembling in harmony with the lower set. Her heaving chest syncs to the rhythm being delivered by my dick, and adoration overwhelms my senses. Every breath taken is only enough to feed the energy it needs to continuously hit her to the hilt. My stare becomes pasted to the point of attachment where her pussy is in the process of stretching over and over again to welcome me. To *worship* me. The sloppy sonance of her soaking state sings like an anthem my soul is devoted to playing for the rest of my goddamn life. Juices drench my tightening sack while sweat builds in the crease of my brow. Despite her obvious desire for me to move faster, I maintain the lowkey tempo, loving the different connection we're displaying.

Loving that we can *make love.*

Loving that we're *in love.*

I groan louder as the emotions invoked over having everything I've always wanted in my life grow stronger.

Amazing job.

Amazing house.

Amazing car.

Even more amazing wife.

Well…soon to be wife.

That ring will be on her finger tonight.

Lenny links her glazed gaze to mine. "Te amo mucho, Papi."

The proclamation takes me by surprise though it shouldn't.

This is who she is.

She's not the overthinker that I am. Not the overplanner. Not the one who has to calculate the likeliness of having the other person say it back, then test the waters with love-related phrases. She lets her feelings guide her. The moment be seized. Life lived.

My forehead drops against her, and I whisper, "Say it again, baby."

"Te amo mucho." Her pussy starts to swell. "Siempre te he amado." Warning quivers of her orgasms increase around my dick. "And I have, Gideon. I've always loved you, and I always will."

The weight of her words combined with the pressure of her pussy pull an orgasm out of me at the same time they do her. "Fuck, I love you too."

There's no time to chastise myself for the lack of couth or romance missing in my response.

Our mouths crash together, tongues imprisoning one another as if terrified this moment is too good to be true. Sweltering surges spill inside, and Lenny's pussy unabashedly gorges on the reward. Trapped moans are released in tandem while we tremble with such momentum the bed threatens to collapse.

Obviously spent, we crumple into a twisted, tangled ball yet leave our lips locked to allow our earlier announcements the chance to be wordlessly repeated.

I'm not entirely sure how I let her slip out of my arms to get dressed to leave.

I'm even less sure how I didn't get out of bed to walk her down to her car.

And I'm absolutely fucking clueless on how I let myself go back to sleep instead of getting up to work on BJ's deal.

It isn't until the sound of my doorbell is pinging around my bedroom that I make any real effort to get the day started.

Yes. Laziness is *unlike* me. But, all things considered, maybe it's okay to occasionally indulge in it. Why should I be the only asshole on the planet who doesn't get to sleep in once in awhile? Why should I fucking sacrifice countless hours of sex and sleep to stress over some teenager who is more concerned with getting his cock touched than he is his future career? Why is it so wrong to swap sitting at my kitchen table for staying snug in the space that still smells like my woman? And why am I not surprised she smells like fresh tortillas?

The doorbell rings again receiving a disapproving grunt in return.

Unsure who it is since I don't recall inviting anyone over, I slip over to the dresser to grab a pair of sleep pants. I scrub my face on the way over and do a breath check in case it is someone slightly important.

Doubt it is. It's probably Mick wondering why my ass isn't in the office today...Like work is the *only* thing that matters in my life.

It doesn't.

And tonight, Lenny will have no doubt about that little fact.

As soon as the door is open, the attractive woman with extremely light brown skin clutching multiple grocery bags lets out a heavy sigh. "Please, tell me you're Gideon Lucas."

I lazily lean one arm against the frame. "I am."

"Perfect! I am *horrible* at following GPS directions, so when you didn't immediately answer I was worried I had the wrong house."

"Pretty sure you still have the wrong house." My head tilts to the side in suspicion. "I have no idea who you are."

"Natalie."

The name rings no bells.

"We met through Connect…"

My eyes begin to bulge.

"I know you most likely only saw my profile picture *once*, which wasn't exactly super helpful since it wasn't just *me* in the photo, but that's what I get for letting my crazy, older, hotter sister set the damn thing up for me. Anyway, we're supposed to be having brunch together today."

"Wait. Wait. Wait." I stand up completely straight and fold my arms across my chest. "Did you not get my email?"

"Don't check my personal email when I'm out of town for work. There's rarely any time. Between buying fresh ingredients and dealing with different kitchen staffs, not to mention clients, I really don't answer anything that's not work-related."

I can't help smiling. "I completely understand."

Which is probably one reason Lenny thought this match was originally a good idea.

After stealing another glance at the heavy grocery bags in her arms, I transfer most of the bags from her possession to mine. "Come on in, and I'll explain everything."

Natalie follows me back into the house, shutting the door behind her. We cross over to the kitchen in silence, although, I know I should say *something*.

Do I offer her gas money for what she unnecessarily spent?

Is it *her* fault for not checking her emails?

Am I still required to let her make me a meal?

We plop the bags on the empty counter space, and she compliments, "This kitchen is beautiful. Everything in it is perfect. The stainless-steel appliances. The crisp modern décor. The dream stove...And don't forget the easy layout for a real cook to work flawlessly in." Her eyes meet mine. "Are you big on cooking?"

My back braces against the island. "I have to be. I'm the only one who typically does it."

If I'm honest with myself I'm not sure that Lenny *can't* so much as she has mastered the art of manipulating me into it.

"Well, that may change..."

Her sly grin sparks me to state, "The email I sent you was to cancel."

"Oh, well, then this is mega awkward." She tries to bat away the redness coloring her cheeks. "Did you completely cancel or reschedule?"

"Cancel."

"Was it something I said or did or somehow managed to spook you in the one email we swapped?"

"No. Not at all. To be totally honest, my girlfriend set this up-"

"*More* mega awkward," she mumbles.

"That sounds bad. Let me start at the beginning," I rush to explain. "Lenny, my girlfriend or more accurately, the woman I'm going to ask to marry me today-"

"*Super* mega awkward."

"-works for Connect. She actually works in the matching department. She's one of the people they use to read the profiles and declare some of the matches."

"That's not all computer-based?"

"To my understanding, a computer makes the initial matches and then actual humans with a brain double check to assure success."

Natalie nods her understanding, bobbed haircut brushing against her face.

"Unfortunately, her small stint in this position kinda inflated her ego to an obnoxious level. She's *not* good at matchmaking. Like at all. Like should've never been hired level of bad. She doesn't seem to understand that just because you're a great therapist doesn't equate to being a great matchmaker."

232

"I could kinda see the correlation."

"In ways so can I, but this whole matchmaker bullshit was more or less her way of hiding from a horrific experience. *I* wasn't fully aware of that when we made our deal-"

"Deal?"

"The deal was, she had seven dates to find me a 'match' aka a woman I wanted to go on a second date with or she had to take a job, a real job, a real job in her field that brought in a salary with benefits as opposed to a paycheck that barely covered rent. What she didn't know was it was an impossible task because for the last fifteen years of our lives, I've been in love with *her*."

Natalie's expression softens.

"I don't know how to explain it, but the moment I saw her do the Hammer Time dance in the middle of a fucking frat party, I just *knew* she was it for me." My shrug is small. "Sadly, she's only gotten better at that dance as time has ticked on." We exchange a couple chuckles. "I *agreed* to this asinine situation simply to do what her stubborn ass has a habit of *not* letting me do, which is *help* her. Really help. And by help, I mean reminding her that just because she had one setback doesn't mean she needed to give up. I wanted her to see that sometimes we just have to switch visions of a dream, not necessarily the dreams themselves."

"That's quite profound."

"Thanks." Another friendly grin appears. "I guess, I just needed her to get out of her own way and was willing to do whatever it took for that to happen. Thinking back on it, we *both* needed to get out of our own ways to see the relationship we had been nurturing for over a decade was much more than just friendship. My only regret, aside from the obvious of waiting this long to get the balls to give us a shot, is the innocent women I went out with in the process.

I knew they never had a shot, but they didn't. *You* didn't. And it was wrong to put any of you in this position."

To my surprise, Natalie offers me a warm hum. "I don't know that that's true."

"What?"

She bounces her shoulders. "Going out with other women, other women you might've been compatible with wasn't necessarily a bad idea. You got to see that there were other options and realize that the *best* option was the one right in front of you. Like you said, you needed to get out of your own way, and I think your twisted dating deal helped with that."

She's right.

Absolutely right.

This woman is attractive, bright, understanding, and cooks.

Hate to admit, but Lenny was onto something here.

"Sorry you were caught up in it," I apologize. "And sorry you brought all this food over for no reason..." My eyes give the groceries another glimpse. "I can write you a check to reimburse you for it. Or I can help you take it back out to your car. Or-"

"I could make you and your girlfriend brunch?" She unexpectedly suggests.

"What?"

"Yeah. You could pay me to make the two of you a romantic brunch. I mean, I am a personal chef with her own successful catering company. It's literally what I do for a living...though typically for athletes and actors and occasionally royalty."

Curiosity gets the better of me. "Athletes?"

"*Usually* catering parties or banquets for them, but every once in awhile, I'll get a weird request to come cook so they can impress a woman they wanna bang or apologize to the woman they are banging for banging someone else."

I smirk at her word choice.

"It'd be nice to make dinner for a normal couple, well, normal relatively speaking."

"You don't think that'd be...*awkward*?"

"You mean *more* awkward than arriving to make a brunch for a half-naked hunk only to find out it was cancelled because he's already in a relationship?"

My cringing is proceeded by peering down at my bare chest.

Fuck me. Have I really been having this long-ass conversation with this woman while practically wearing nothing?

Why didn't that hit me sooner?

Why don't I feel uncomfortable or self-conscious about it?

Is this a good thing or bad thing?

Did Lenny know this woman would be this easy for me to be around?

Why is she this easy to be around?

"Besides, if I'm being honest, I fucking *love* cooking in new kitchens. It's my not so secret obsession. I love the thrill of the discovery." She bites down onto her bottom lip in excitement. "My absolute favorite thing is when I'm wandering around and working in a new environment while *RoboCop* plays in the background on my tablet."

My mouth goes agape. "Are you fucking serious? *RoboCop* is your favorite movie, too?"

"Of *all* time. Like if I have a kid, I wanna name him Alex or Murphy or Alex Murphy, not as a first and middle name, but as his hyphenated first name."

Holy shit, I've had similar conversations with Lenny about that!

Is this woman *for real*? Is she an actual person or an actress my girlfriend hired to test me?

That's not something Lenny would do, is it? That requires a lot of extra thoughts and planning, not two things she does an over the top amount of.

"The first *RoboCop* was incredible, however, the remake? Makes me violent just thinking about it."

"Thank you!"

"Why did they find the need to ruin a classic? Why do they always find the need to ruin *classics*?"

"I cannot tell you how many times I've gone on this exact tangent with Lenny."

Natalie begins unloading items from the sacks. "The woman you're going to propose to?"

My blush immediate. "Yes."

"What's a better way to start the day of proposal than with an exotic spread of crêpes both sweet and savory made completely from

236

scratch?" She inches over a bit to reach for another bag. "And instead of listening to my all-time favorite movie, I will listen to you tell me all about what I'm sure is an amazing woman considering the check you're about to cut."

Chuckles creep up the back of my throat. "Are we talking an arm or a leg?"

"Both." Natalie's body brushes mine. "Probably a testicle too."

This time we both laugh loudly.

"I'm clearly interrupting," Lenny's voice says with hints of sadness caked to it.

Our attention immediately soars to where she's standing at the kitchen's edge.

Her attire isn't what I was imagining it would be. Most of the interviews she's gone to, I had to twist her arm into wearing something more professional, something I knew would impress who was going to hire or not hire her, yet the sleek, black business dress she has on now indicates all my lectures didn't fall on deaf ears. They were just waiting for the right opportunity to be put to the best use.

It's about timing.

Everything is about timing…

And this is shitty fucking time.

"Now *this* is the epitome of mega awkward," Natalie mutters under her breath.

"I should go." My girlfriend doesn't linger around for an explanation. She spins on her black high heels that I'm starting to wonder why I've never seen before and bolts for the front door.

"Lenny wait!"

Rushing out after her proves to be necessary. The speed at which she vanishes from the kitchen yet reappears at the doorway is alarming.

We've been friends for most of our lives, and I don't think I've ever seen her move so fucking fast.

Not even when her favorite taco truck is getting ready to pull out of its spot, and it's clear we are too late to be customers.

"Lenny wait!"

"No," she denies, opening the front door.

"Come on, Lenny! It's not what it looks like!"

The words cause her to turn to face me though she continues to back up. "It's *always* what it looks like because we're not in a movie!"

My mouth twitches to argue but isn't granted the chance.

"You don't have to explain," she states matter of factly. "I get it."

Bafflement burrows into my expression.

Lenny opens her car door with a rough yank. "Between last night and saying I love you this morning...it was all too much, too fast."

"Wh-"

"You probably weren't expecting any of it and just didn't know how to fucking say this was just something good to do until something better came along."

"Len-"

"And I get it. I *know* Natalie's a better pick, Gideon. I fucking picked her! Same hobbies! Same favorite movies! Same love of expensive food!"

I'm not given room for a rebuttal.

"You even deal with the same *clients*! You're on similar career paths and even have a tendency to travel to the same places! She is clearly the better match here, so do yourself a favor and go back in there and finish whatever it is you were *clearly*," her hand gestures towards my bare chest, "in the middle of. Or go for a second round, I guess."

"Len-"

She shuts the door with her inside, cutting off the rest of her name.

My instinct to run over and stand stubbornly behind her car clashes with the logical decision to stay where I am in the middle of my yard. Part of me wants to the make the giant dramatic stop of her vehicle. Scream. Shout. Demand she listen to what it is I have to say. However, the other part of me is convinced running around in my pajamas in broad daylight would be terrible for my image. For business. That that's not the man who is tasked with convincing what could be the next Wayne Gretzky to let him be his agent.

A familiar uncertainty crawls through my veins.

Maybe I should just give her a minute to cool down?

Maybe I should wait and see if she comes back?

Maybe I should call her again and again until she gives me an actual moment to explain how wrong she is about everything?

Like usual, Lenny makes the decision for the both of us. She backs out of the driveaway without offering me another glance.

How the fuck did I go from having *everything* to wondering if I have *anything* at all in a matter of seconds?

chapter twelve

Lennox

Got the dream job yet lost the dream guy.

Sounds about right.

Heaven fucking forbid the scales of goodness ever weigh too heavily to one side for *me*.

The sniffling man in front of me snatches my thoughts back from their own private pity party.

"It's not that I don't love my son," Ronald states quietly.

"Then what is it?!" His wife, Rhonda, snaps.

"I don't *trust* myself alone around him!"

Knowing the importance of letting emotions explode in safe settings, I don't advise him to calm down or lower his tone. I allow him the space to stretch out what it is he fears he can't under his own roof.

"What if I have...an *episode*?" His choice of phrasing regarding the harsher moments of his PTSD is one we're all familiar with.

I helped them come together to create a code for it.

Something they could say without telling the whole world what was happening when they were in public.

Something they could *share* in understanding without the negative stain that the abbreviation tends to lead to.

"What if I'm holding our son...our barely three-month-old son and I just drop him?" Ronald's eyes begin to water. "Or throw him? What if a flashback hits me right then, and I think he's something he isn't? What if I accidentally harm him the one time we're alone together?"

Her hands fly to her face as if uncertain what to say.

I gingerly investigate, "Are the medications they prescribed not working?"

He hesitates to nod. "They are but..." Ronald bobs his head back and forth. "What if they *stop*? What if-"

"You cannot play the what if game," I snip a little harsher than intended. "You cannot *live* a life constantly asking, 'what if'. That's not living. That's spectating. That's...*observing*. That's missing the moments you left the military for because you were tired of missing."

Both people focus their stares on me.

"I'm not saying I don't understand your fears or your concerns." My voice regains its compassion. "I'm not saying you're in the wrong for having them. I'm simply reminding you that you cannot continue to lead a *healthy*, *active*, *involved* life if you let them *cripple* you again. Those fears kept you from initially dating, remember?"

"And then you met *me*," Rhonda interjects, hand landing on his forearm.

His fingers lock with hers. "Your presence just silences everything else."

God, I hate them so hard right now.

I sit up in my broken office chair and fidget with the closest object in reach. "You were worried she would never understand what it was you went through, that she would shun you once she realized you had a condition, yet she never did. She stayed by your side through all the appointments. Through all the paperwork. Through all *these* visits. Do you remember when you two came for pre-marital counseling the night before your wedding because you were afraid you'd have an episode in church?"

Ronald slowly nods.

"What did I tell you then?"

"The same thing you're telling me now."

My free hand tosses itself slightly into the air. "Take what you consider is a risk to bond with your son. Perhaps you build up to being left alone. Start with allowing Rhonda to take a long bath while you watch Rupert. Then maybe while she goes to the grocery store. Then maybe while she goes out with friends to dinner. Build up to the level you two want to be at, but don't be ashamed that it may be a slower process. Don't be ashamed that you may need to pace yourself and take it day by day. Can we try that? Can we try building towards the same end goal?"

Ronald's nodding is much quicker.

I divert my stare to his wife. "Well?"

"I would love that. Hell, just hearing the word bath sounds incredible."

My smile is instant. "I completely understand that."

Because it does. A nice long bubble bath, an Old Fashion, and *Clueless* rolling in the background sounds like the perfect weekend activity. Unfortunately, I will probably be settling for crying on my couch, taking shots of tequila out of the bottle, and yelling at the bitch that let Leo drown. There was enough room for both of them on that door. He should've lived! *They* should've lived! It should've been one more amazing love story to the roster of '90's classics instead of the brutal burden that is to only be watched when I need a good, long, ugly bawl fest.

The couple exchanges loving hand squeezes followed by sweet chaste kisses.

Not cringing is so difficult I accidentally snap my crayon in half.

It's not that I don't want *others* to be happy…

Or in love.

Or building a beautiful future.

I'm not one of those people that really feels misery needs company but watching two people find peace after spending the previous day, evening, and night cycling through emotions like they were stretches of a Triathlon because my boyfriend…er…guy friend I made the mistake of admitting I was in love with, decided he wasn't done searching for something better, is excruciatingly harder than it's ever been before. But it'll get easier once I give myself adequate time to…move forward.

Which is what I need to do.

Even if I have no clue *how* to do it.

Thankfully, Ronald and Rhonda are my last clients of the day. I make the decision to ditch the normal lingering around I would do to go shopping for new office décor. While I wanted that to be something Gideon and I did together today since he is the king of sophistication and would love celebrating my new job by splurging, I'll have to settle for doing it alone. Like many more things that are to come.

244

Just as I throw my bag over my shoulder, there's a knock on my office door.

The visitor doesn't wait for permission to enter.

Gideon simply walks in, shuts the door behind, and states, "I'm here to talk."

"I'm not here to listen."

He winces at the venom spewed. "But that's your job."

"Si, for the great men and women who have served this nation and the family members they need to come in with them for support." My fingers tighten around the strap. "You are not one of those people."

"Correct, but I am a person in crisis," he tempts. "And *you* would never just abandon someone who was clearly in need."

"Need of what, exactly?"

"Relationship advice."

Fuck, one date with the woman who was practically built *for him* in some weird futuristic factory and they're already in a relationship?!

I grunt at the response. "I'm all out of it today, but I'll give you the card of someone you can talk to."

"No," Gideon argues. "I wanna talk to *you* about *us*."

"There is no us. You made that abundantly clear-"

245

"No, *you* made that abundantly clear," he bites and takes a step towards me. "*You* walked away from me. Not the other way around."

My bag hits the floor with a giant thud. "Are you fucking serious right now?" I advance in his direction. "*You* gave up on us long before I walked out that door! *You* have always had one foot in and apparently one foot out! *You-*"

"Don't fucking try to put this all on me, Lennox!" His use of my full name stops me in my tracks. "I am not the only one who couldn't find the fucking courage to just do what the fuck it is I've wanted to do for most of my adult life! I am not the only one who had to hide behind some fucked up concordance in order to experience what it is I have wasted so much time *dreaming* about. And I damn sure am not the one who didn't even take a minute to *hear* what the other person had to say when the time truly mattered!"

"Oír?!" My voice hits new high notes. "The words coming out of your mouth would've been in direct conflict to the ones your body was saying! More importantly, you lied to me!"

"I didn't lie to you!"

"You did! You said you were done dating, yet I go away for a few hours to an interview, and you sneak one in?!"

Gideon's hands curls at his sides. "I can explain."

"I don't *want* excuses, Gideon. I don't want something that's a *version* of the truth. I don't want-"

"It's not just about what *you* want, Lennox."

My jaw cracks open.

"*That's* how we fucking got here."

Confusion clouds my expression.

"The shit between us is always off balance. It's always about doing what's best for one side or the other. It's been like that for years. We've always been trying to do what's best for one another instead of what's best for *us*."

I fold my arms firmly across my chest.

"Relationships are about give and take. You know that better than anyone."

"I do."

"Well, in our friendship, you did most of the giving, and I did most of the taking. And in this bizarre bet equivalent, I did most of the giving while you did most of the taking. I let you call the shots. Lead the way. Decide how fast we go and when we stop, despite the fact stopping was never on my roster. If we're gonna do this, it should be a better balance. It shouldn't just be having tacos every night any more than it should be *you* only wanting to talk when *you* wanna talk. You should be willing to stand and *listen*. And I should be willing to run and yell." He momentarily pauses. "I realized that a little too late yesterday, which is why I'm *here* now instead of at the office trying to rewrite the BJ deal."

The response is second nature, "OG, you *need* to be working on that deal."

"No. I *need* to be closing this one."

His choice in metaphor crinkles my brow.

"*You*, Lennox Marston, are the most important person in my life. Being with you…*really* being with you is the only thing I give a fuck about. Whether that means I have to spend the next fifteen years waiting for another opportunity for us to be together or just fifteen more minutes to explain that Natalie, the chef, didn't receive the email I sent to cancel, so she showed up anyway and then *stayed* to make you a congratulations breakfast for a *very high fee*, I'm prepared to do it. I'm open to negotiating where we live, what we eat, and whose family we spend which holidays with, but I am not giving up on us. That's not up for debate. Not now. Not ever again."

My heart pounds harshly against my chest. "You weren't…on a date with another woman the morning you finally said you loved me?"

He shakes his head.

"Then why were you-"

"In just sleep pants? Natalie woke me up by ringing the doorbell. Turns out making love to the woman I wanna spend forever with was exhausting."

"Right? I almost fell asleep brushing my teeth."

Hints of mirth creep into our eyes.

"What about," my arms wiggle in the position, "the closeness? The flirting-"

"We were *talking*," he promptly corrects. "She was just that easy to get along with, a lot like you."

His statement returns the discomfort.

"That was the major problem with every woman you threw my way."

"Huh?"

"They were *like you*, but they weren't *you*. And I don't want some new-to-the-league rookie when I can have the hall of fame champion."

My lip becomes imprisoned by my teeth.

"You overreacted yesterday. I underreacted. There's so much new shit for us to figure out that learning the right way to respond is going to take some time, which I'm fine with as long as we're crystal clear about one thing forward."

"What's that?"

"Trust."

The word screeches like nails on a chalkboard.

"We have to trust each other, Lennox, or this will only end in flames. And you know that."

"I do. I just-"

"Overreacted."

"Si! But, I mean, come on! You were practically naked with a gorgeous woman strutting around your kitchen just hours after I left!"

"It was by no means my intention, something you would've known had you given me the chance to explain as opposed to declaring *for me* who I wanted to be with."

I drop my arms and softly sigh. "Lo siento."

A teasing smirk touches his lips. "Could you repeat that for me in English, please. My Spanish isn't as good as it used to be."

"Yeah, neither's your football fling."

"Hey!" He points a playful finger at me. "I got back in the zone! Shit was tied before our Godson was ready to meet us."

Reflecting back to the life-changing moment, I cautiously question, "So none of that shit freaked you out? You weren't...panicking or trying to make sure being with me was the right decision by checking out the last woman I picked out for you?"

Gideon shakes his head. "Being with you has always and will always be the right decision, Lenny."

Relief allows my smile to beam bright.

"Now," he closes the distance between us, "we should probably talk about one more thing."

"What's that?"

He fishes a note out of his pants pocket and hands it to me.

Unsure of what it could be, I hastily unfold it to see something written in familiar red lipstick that stuns me silent.

Will you marry me?

My eyes dart to where he was standing yet is now kneeling. "Lenny..."

He's not actually going to...

"I'm gonna need an answer to that message." Gideon pulls out a ring box from his jacket pocket. "And pretty quick since we have celebration reservations at Lupe Del Rio for a late lunch."

His confidence is too hard not to poke. "What if I say no?"

"Then we tuck this bad boy back into my pocket until a later date and just celebrate the job offer I know you got."

"Oh my god, I *did* get it."

Gideon grins and opens the box. "You took one offer. Take this one too."

My eyes steal a glimpse of the rose gold, diamond halo engagement ring despite the fact I don't really care what it looks like. I leave him hanging on for only a moment longer. "Si."

He doesn't move as if uncertain he heard correctly. "Now in English."

"Why? You know enough Spanish to know what I'm saying."

"Yes, but I wanna know you're gonna spend the rest of your life with me in *both* languages."

I girlishly giggle at the same time I nod. "Yes, OG. I will marry you."

"*Only Gideon*," he announces during his removal of the ring from the box. "That's what OG will stand for from this point forward."

"That's what it's always stood for."

A possessive groan is grabbed, and he quickly pushes the object in place.

The moment he's on his feet our mouths meld together in unmirrored joy.

Maybe Gideon was right.

Maybe I was a shitty matchmaker.

251

Maybe I just ended up getting people laid rather than helping them fall in love.

Whatever the case may be, there's no denying there's one match I did help make, and it's without a doubt the one that matters most.

epilogue

About four years later...

Gideon

This is ridiculous. How is it this responsibility always falls on me? There are *two* of us in this situation, yet someway, somehow it always ends up being *me* who has to do this part.

I swear, I gotta figure out a way to combat their big beautiful brown eyes from doing this to me.

"Incoming," I announce as I arrive at our row.

"Ooo," Jesse, our adopted nine-year-old squeaks. "Nachos! Gimme! Gimme!"

"Tus modales," Lenny fusses at the same time she begins helping hand out the items. "Besides, *those* have jalapenos, those are clearly for *mom*."

Jesse tries not to frown. "Is that cotton candy only for you, too?"

"Dad, did you get me a corndog?" Oscar, our twelve-year-old, grumps from his end seat.

"I got everyone's orders."

All the eyes of my family land on me.

It's still insane to believe most days.

Lenny and I have a *family*. An actual family.

We got married about a month after our engagement and spending time with our Godchild, honorary nieces, and *actual* nieces and nephews got us to wanting to expand ours. Fostering was a planned but difficult route. We went to classes. Opted to foster siblings, which is a harder situation to endure, and were eventually allowed to officially adopt them.

Jesse and Oscar are polar opposites despite their obvious resemblance to one another. They're both of Dominican descent. Both lanky with brown eyes and thick brown hair. But, where she is upbeat, social, and very much into what I do for a living, he's withdrawn, quiet, and has difficulty speaking to anyone besides Lenny, which honestly hurts as his father. My wife, my lovely, loud, let him do his own thing wife, however, does her best to coach me into being the man *he* needs. It's a strange concept to me that two siblings could ever need to be treated different ways for anything other than gender. I often have to follow Lenny's lead, and that is also frustrating because I feel like I should be doing better than I am. Shouldn't parenting come naturally, like learning a new sport?

"Grab your stuff," I state to my wife, hating the way we have to censor ourselves.

Part of that is related to Rainne and Alexander repeating curse words they heard us say during game night. The other is not wanting our kids tossing them out before we're ready.

She slips out her nachos then hands Jesse hers. "Heck yes! Extra cheese!" Jesse turns her Hellcats cap backwards causing her to look more like her mother. "Dad, have I mentioned how much I love you?"

"Not today." My teasing is proceeded with handing her bright blue cotton candy and eventually Oscar his corndog. "However, the day ain't over."

"This game might as well be," Oscar complains as I sit down between him and his sister. "Why doesn't the other team just quit? The Hellcats are killing them."

"You don't just *quit* because you're losing," I start to explain. "I mean, your mom does."

"Disculpa! Don't you dare pretend like you don't magically turn off the video game when my points are getting too high!"

Oscar frowns at me "Wait, that's *not* an accident?"

Thought losing to Lenny was humiliating enough until my death metal-loving, only wears black, somehow we bond over basketball, son schooled me in every game we play together. I'll admit it. My pride gets in the way. Can't let your son come out of the gate kicking your ass. That's just rules of the jungles. It'd be like letting a junior agent negotiate a bigger contract than me, something that has *never* or *will ever* happen.

Initially, the deal with BJ wasn't made. My decision to propose to my best friend instead of devote time to an athlete that wasn't ready spooked Barrett Gallagher. Mick was pissed but understood what I did and respected it. The missed deal with BJ, however, had a silver lining. One of his elite teammates on his year-round team wanted representation. Turns out he was more serious than BJ and much more anxious to learn. His parents understood what it would take and quickly jumped on the opportunity for representation. Thanks to my guidance, he was drafted by the NHL at eighteen and traded to the Highland team at nineteen. Since being in the league, he's made quite a name and rank for himself. BJ, on the other hand, ended up playing for an overseas team. It's one of those rare moments where *not* making the deal was better.

Negotiating with the love of my life was the only thing I needed to be doing that weekend. Supporting *her*. Being there for *her* and *her career*. She loves working with couples full-time but still loves her time at the Veteran clinic. To no surprise, both of our hours have had to be cut back in order to give our family what it needs to stay strong. I travel less. Either go in early or come home later, never both. Lenny mirrors the time so we are whole and not loving the kids in a divided nature. We've learned we have to be co-coaches on everything from what we serve for dinner to not letting Oscar have a girlfriend.

In the bigger picture of everything, that's what we've always been.

A dream team.

Except now instead of doing it to sign deals or woo athletes or impress old college pals, we do it to build a great support system for our family.

For the next generation who has to tackle the world by storm.

For our son and daughter who will know your fractured past doesn't have to fuck up your future, and that regardless of what the world thinks, the only dreams that matter are the ones you're willing to chase…

And that's what a life with Lenny will always be to me.

She is the dream I am always willing to chase.

The match I'm glad she eventually made.

The deal I'm most thankful to have signed.

Did you enjoy this novel?

Please leave a review!

Other Works

Wondering about how Jaye and Archer got their start?

Check out the standalone novel

Compassion

Jaye Jenkins is dealing with the death of her fiancé, an overbearing mother, and an awkward social existence when a green-eyed stranger stumbles into her life. For some reason she can't stop thinking about the mysterious man she knows she has no right to be fantasizing about. Suddenly, an uncontrollable situation occurs, and in a single moment, one simple act of kindness changes everything.

https://amzn.to/2N7ImJ0

Remember the online dating company Lenny worked for?

Check out a relationship it *successfully* started…

Walking Away

JASON

For her sake I should walk away. I'm not the man she needs.

GWEN

For his sake I should walk away. I'm not the one he wants.

HUDSON

For their sake I should walk away. I'm not the solution. I'm a new problem.

What happens when three people unexpectedly fall in love and one should walk away, but can't?

*PLEASE NOTE: This is an M/M/F STANDALONE NOVEL.

https://amzn.to/2TQfUxF

Curious about Heath's daughter?

Meet her in her own trilogy!

King's Return (Camelot Misfits #1)

Chivalry isn't dead.

It just rides a motorcycle now...

The Misfits MC is known for maintaining the balance.

Providing common ground.

Protecting the innocent.

However, when Adonis "King" Arthur is forced to return home to help rescue a fellow member's sister from a rival club, he quickly realizes the place he held in his memory as a haven is anything but....

*WARNING: This book ends on a CLIFFHANGER.

This is book 1 of 3 for King and Imani.

https://amzn.to/2DE6RJf

Interested in a story about Carly?

She has her own too!

Redneck Romeo (The Culture Blind Series #1)

A small town man.

A big city woman.

A star-crossed love affair that begins in paradise...

What starts as five days of fun in the sun leads to two people traveling down an emotional dirt road.

Down a highway paved with good intentions but full of unpredicted roadblocks.

Will the tumultuous track they take ultimately tear them apart, leaving their lives in a tattered tragedy, or will they manage to survive and tie their souls together for a life time?

* Complete Standalone *

https://amzn.to/2TOZVQp

Did you know famous Cooper Copeland, the country singer, has his own book!

Cowboy Casanova (The Culture Blind Series #2)

A country music king.

A chess playing queen.

A classic tale that begins in paradise...

What starts as an annual five day music festival on the beach leads to two people falling in love with new rhythms.

Opposites anxiously trying to learn the beats of one another's hearts.

Will the endless noise of one industry ultimately tear them apart, leaving their relationship to be nothing more than a forgotten melody, or will they manage to survive and create their perfect harmony?

* This book is a COMPLETE standalone. The Culture Blind Series can be read in any order *

https://amzn.to/2TRv59S

How about a book about another Clover Rose Alum?

The Substitute (The Bro Series #1)

Nate

Being a substitute teacher is good for me.
It's sensible.
Logical.
Abandoning my plans for a career in the film industry and a life full of fun, albeit slightly reckless, actions was the responsible thing to do.
That's who I am now.
That's who I've become.
Mr. Boring. Mr. Predictable. Mr. Anal Retentive.
At least that's what I thought until one irresistible student breathes life back into the version of me I've been desperately trying to suffocate.
Being with Ainsley isn't a want. It's a need.
And I'm willing do anything to fulfill it.

Ainsley

I've spent my entire life ashamed of who I am.
Who my mother is. What she does.
Being forced to attend a private school where people endlessly whisper about it is only bearable because I know exactly what's in my future.
I know exactly where I'm going.
I know exactly what to do to get there.
Or at least I thought I did.
One class with him and suddenly my entire world was missing one very important piece.
Being with Nate isn't just about sex.
It's about loving life in a way I never imagined.
The situation isn't ideal, but I'll do whatever it takes to be with him.
https://amzn.to/2EbbZGk

There's another Drake Lenzi fan who has his novel!

The Hacker (The Bro Series #2)

HOLDEN

Life is nothing more than a series of 1s and 0s.

Basic choices.

Yes or no.

Fight or flight.

Protect or neglect.

Pack or prey.

Felon or free.

I've mastered the art of when to hit 1 and when to hit 0.

Or at least I had before Meena came back into my world.

Now, I'm constantly confused which one to hit.

Somehow she's hacked my system and rewritten my code to become one of the only people in my life who matters.

One of the only people I wouldn't hesitate to die for.

Loving her has become an involuntary 1.

Like protecting my children.

Like breathing.

MEENA

Temporary.

Everything in life is just temporary.

Unlike most people, I choose to acknowledge that.

Embrace it.

Make the most of a situation for what it is and then move on.

It makes what I do for a living easier.

It makes dating simple.

Or at least it had before I crossed paths again with the only man who has ever made me crave something permanent.

Too bad Holden wasn't mine then.

Too bad I can't be his forever now.

He'll never completely move on from her.

He'll never completely let go.

Loving him is a constant I'm trying to shake.

Unfortunately, I'm not sure I ever will.

https://amzn.to/2InxyaC

How about a book about someone else who loves the coffee shop, Loco Moco?

The Suit (The Bro Series #3)

PAXTON

I'm not supposed to mix business with pleasure.
Confuse sex with commitment.
Cross my past with my future.
Let the man I am mingle with the man I have always wanted to be.
These are the simple guidelines I live by.
The principles I mentally enforce.
But after I steal a taste of the wrong woman, there's only one rule that matters.
Protect Ryann and her daughter at all costs.

RYANN

Being a mom is what defines me.
I'm no longer the risk taker I once was.
The cigar and whiskey wild child.
A confident woman intrigued by the future rather than fearful of it.
That is until Paxton rewrites everything I knew about life.
About men.
About myself.
He just wants a real chance to love us, but I'm afraid our lives will ruin his.
https://amzn.to/2DBWTYY

The popular Wilcox Whiskey Brand belongs to a billionaire with quite a story…

Private (Private Series #1)

Mogul or Monster?

Billionaire Weston Wilcox hasn't been seen by the outside world in almost a decade. No face to face meetings. No interviews. No social media accounts. Despite his ghost demeanor he continues to financially flourish and make his fellow investors richer with every decision. Throughout the years many have sought to discover the man inside the mogul while others have spread legends painting him as a heartless monster consumed by greed. None of it matters to him. Weston's true identity is secured away in his estate of solitude, which consists of the only people in the entire world he believes he can trust. That is until he's asked to allow a guest access to the property under extreme circumstances. One he knows he shouldn't. It doesn't take long before his world is turned upside down, unexpected threats arise, and Weston's forced to ask himself what really should be kept private?

https://amzn.to/2TRxQYM

The owner of Runt's Beer has his own book too!

Must Love Hogs (Must Love Series #1)

Thirty.

Single.

And apparently a pig parent in a custody battle...

Olivia "Ollie" Steele isn't expecting to take care of the pet pig her ex boyfriend randomly leaves behind, but when a handsome, green eyed stranger comes by demanding custody, she absolutely refuses to let go of her new pink pal. Never mind that she lives in a downtown city apartment or that she's not sure if pigs are on the approved pet list. Her stubbornness causes the two of them to start an unusual friendship. Before either has a chance to overthink the many, many reasons why they shouldn't fall in love, they do.

Can these two opposites make it work or will Ollie end up exactly where she started?

Thirty.

Single.

And a pig parent in a custody battle.
https://amzn.to/2DCE5c6

Big L, the owner of the Hellcats basketball team has a daughter!

Her standalone story is fun and sports filled…

Must Love Pogs (Must Love Series #3)

Thirty.

Single.

And always wanted for the wrong reasons...

London "Little L" Hall is considered sports royalty to most people, but when the sexy, blue eyed stranger she rescues at an event admits he's never heard of her or her famous father, she can't help herself from being interested. It doesn't matter that they are hardly compatible. It doesn't matter that he cringes at her eccentric taste in clothing and music, while she frowns at his obsessive cleaning and pretentious food choices. Falling in love with one another is easy and exciting.

However, when the relationship gets challenged, will they come out on the same side or will London end up exactly where she started?

Thirty.

Single.

And always wanted for the wrong reasons.

https://amzn.to/2Ear9eT

Interested in learning more about the famous actor they saw karaoke?

Check out that scene and more in this standalone novel.

Already Designed (The South Haven Crew #1)

When laid-back Hollywood heartthrob, Levi Stone, asks Kadence Allan out for a date he isn't expecting to be rejected.

He isn't expecting to have to practically beg for a chance.

He isn't expecting to be challenged every time she opens her mouth.

Most importantly, he isn't expecting how hard he's willing to work at being Mr. Right rather than Mr. Right Now.

Can Levi convince Kadence he's worth the risk of rearranging her entire life to include him, or will she stick to the plans she's already designed?

https://amzn.to/2If8JxC

Remember Gideon's date who loved motorcycle tricks?

She's not the only one around who loves them!

Meet the McCoys to find out more.

Classic (The Adrenaline Series #1)

Boy meets girl. Girl meets boy. They fall in love and live happily ever after, right? That is unless boy is a criminal and girl is the daughter of the man trying to catch him. With circumstances this unforgiving, is there anyway their love story will have an ending that we've come to know as classic?

Warning: Cliffhanger. This is the first in the series

NOW FREE on MOST RETAILERS!

https://amzn.to/2STaMeX

Gratitude:

The list of people who allow this entire process is truly too many to name. So rather than run the risk of forgetting anyone, I want to just say thank you to EVERYONE. Readers, bloggers, friends, family, reviewers, and street teamers....you are all matches I am glad I have found. I can't thank you enough for sticking around over the years, but I most definitely will continue to try.

Until next time…

FOLLOW ME!!!

Facebook
https://www.facebook.com/XavierNealAuthorPage

Facebook Group
https://www.facebook.com/groups/1471618443081356/

Twitter
@XavierNeal87

Instagram
@xavierneal87

Bookbub
https://www.bookbub.com/authors/xavier-neal

Goodreads
https://www.goodreads.com/author/show/4990135.Xavier_N
eal

Pintrest
https://www.pinterest.com/xavierneal/

Newsletter Sign up
http://eepurl.com/bYqwLf

More Books By Me

Standalones

Compassion (Military Romance) - https://amzn.to/2FZnxPj

Cinderfella (YA Contemporary) - https://amzn.to/2pBHZff

The Gamble (Romantic Comedy) - https://amzn.to/2uf4ZFw

Freeform (Romantic Comedy) - https://amzn.to/2IPna7W

Part of The List (Contemporary Romance) - https://amzn.to/2udYwuz

Walking Away (Contemporary Ménage Romance) - https://amzn.to/2pAOEGf

Senses Series
(Sports Romance/ Romantic Comedy)

Vital (Prequel Novella)- FREE ON ALL PLATFORMS https://amzn.to/2ueL5KJ

Blind- https://amzn.to/2GmEMcO

Deaf- https://amzn.to/2IK71Rf

Numb- https://amzn.to/2pAOYVt

Hush- https://amzn.to/2pzV2gS

Savor- https://amzn.to/2HZsVP1

Callous- https://amzn.to/2pAPmTV

Agonize- https://amzn.to/2ILLaZw

Suffocate - https://amzn.to/2GjLU9T

Mollify- https://amzn.to/2GgRJoJ

Blur- https://amzn.to/2pD1rrK

Blear - https://amzn.to/2DQGb6a

Senses Box Set (Books 1-5) - https://amzn.to/2Gkxruw

Adrenaline Series

(Romance/ Romantic Suspense)
Classic- https://amzn.to/2I0wd4D   -FREE ON MOST PLATFORMS

Vintage- https://amzn.to/2HXksMw

Masterpiece- https://amzn.to/2G0tWKj

Unmask- https://amzn.to/2Gn2tBK

Error- https://amzn.to/2pBakC6

Iconic- https://amzn.to/2G1Q8Ua

Box Set (Books 1-3) - https://amzn.to/2IP7GRe

Prince of Tease Series

(Romance/ Romantic Comedy)

Prince Arik- https://amzn.to/2pAuhbF

Prince Hunter- https://amzn.to/2IKzuGu

Prince Brock- https://amzn.to/2ufmghN

Prince Chance- https://amzn.to/2LuclMw

Prince Zane- TBA

Hollywood Exchange Series

(Romance/ Romantic Comedy)

Already Written - https://amzn.to/2G0F2ix

Already Secure- TBA

Already Designed (The South Haven Crew #1) - https://amzn.to/2G8A0fP

Already Scripted (The South Haven Crew #2) - TBA

Already Legal (The South Haven Crew #3) - TBA

Already Driven (The South Haven Crew #4) - TBA

Already Cast (The South Haven Crew #5) - TBA

Blue Dream Duet

(Contemporary Romance) (Complete Series)

Blue Dream- https://amzn.to/2Gl296E

Purple Haze- https://amzn.to/2ILKUK2

Havoc Series

(Military Romance/ Romantic Suspense) (Complete Series)

Havoc- FREE ON ALL PLATFORMS - https://amzn.to/2HYWOyZ

Chaos - https://amzn.to/2ug1Ox5

Insanity- https://amzn.to/2I3eABs

Collapse - https://amzn.to/2G3cAww

Devastate- https://amzn.to/2IO9GcL

Havoc Box Set (Books 1-3) - https://amzn.to/2G17519

Never Say Neverland Series

(YA/NA Fantasy Adventure)

Get Lost- https://amzn.to/2G2p3jO

Lost in Lies- https://amzn.to/2IPn7ZO

Lies, Mistrust, and Fairy Dust- https://amzn.to/2pDcpgQ

Dust to Ashes- TBA

Rub Me Series

(Erotic Shorts) (Complete)

Rub Me The Right Way- https://amzn.to/2pFWLkm

Rub Me The Wrong Way- https://amzn.to/2pAf1Wm

Rub Me All The Way- https://amzn.to/2INntQH

Box Set- https://amzn.to/2uflEZx

The Just Series

(Second Chance Romance)

Just Out of Reach- https://amzn.to/2ubzfBe

Just So Far Away- https://amzn.to/2DR57KM

Private Series

(Romantic Suspense)

Private - https://amzn.to/2IN7P7R

Public- https://amzn.to/2pAF7it

Personal- TBA

Duched Series

(Romantic Comedy) (Complete Series)

Duched- https://amzn.to/2G4Xlim

Royally Duched- https://amzn.to/2pAnvDh

Royally Duched Up- https://amzn.to/2G089SP

Duched Deleted (FREE Novella ON ALL PLATOFRMS)-
https://amzn.to/2GlOQTy

The Bros Series

(Erotic Romance) (Complete)

The Substitute- https://amzn.to/2ub9CAc

The Hacker- https://amzn.to/2FZFxJr

The Suit- https://amzn.to/2poTcyX

The Chef- https://amzn.to/2Dgi7MR

Must Love Series

(Sweet, Romantic Comedy)

Must Love Hogs- https://amzn.to/2IMmmkg

Must Love Jogs- https://amzn.to/2pBIiqp

Must Love Pogs- https://amzn.to/2ueUUIu

Must Love Logs- Coming April/May 2019

Must Love Flogs- Coming Soon

The Culture Blind Series

(Contemporary Romance)

Redneck Romeo- https://amzn.to/2vYuPhM

Cowboy Casanova- https://amzn.to/2sxwqGT

Camelot Misfits Series

(MC Romance/ Romantic Suspense)

King's Return - https://amzn.to/2TTnNCl

King's Conquest - https://amzn.to/2IaYZo8

King's Legacy – COMING SOON

Made in the USA
Columbia, SC
25 March 2019